The Magical Secret of the Crystal Kingdom

By P.S. Nicholls

2018

The Magical Secret of the Crystal Kingdom

By P.S. Nicholls

2018

Preface

In a world full of challenges we sometimes lose sight of the magic that is all around us, especially if we are dealing with the loss of something or someone that we love. We can become scared or angry and sometimes even lose hope. This book was inspired by my own experience of feeling overcome with sadness and realising that in my darkest time that life can still be magical.

My beautiful children Rose and George have been a source of constant inspiration, laughter and love in my life. Together we created The Magical Secret of the Crystal Kingdom and it is our hope that this book will bring a smile to many faces, adults and children alike. A reminder to never give up hope and to always dream big.

There are many people who without them, this book would not have been possible and I wish to thank everyone for their help and support along the way. I'm going to give a special mention to my family and close friends for all of the wonderful experiences and lessons that have come my way throughout my life. It has been a life full of love and really at the end of the day that is what life is all about.

This book is dedicated to living a life of love and smiles, to those living and to those we have temporarily lost. We are always with you and you are always with us.

Finally I would like to make a special mention to LPS and ID. You know who you are. Thank you for the Pixie Dust.

With Love,

Paul xxx

The Magical Secret of the Crystal Kingdom

By P.S. Nicholls

2018

Chapter 1 - The Dream

'Welcome home' the lion had been saying over and over again. It normally just looked at her like it was waiting for something to happen. What was going to happen?

Rose was sure that she had never had a dream quite like this before. Flying horses and talking lions, whatever next! It seemed as though she was always dreaming of animals in one way or another but this was the first time they had been flying, or talking for that matter. How exciting it would be if these dreams could be real, even just part of this dream coming true would certainly be amazing. Of course, she didn't know at that point just how amazing it would be and it certainly wasn't the first time that something she had dreamed of, had come true.

She opened her eyes, blinked three times and looked around her room, lying still for a few minutes, letting it all sink in. Everything seemed normal. Pink duvet, pink wallpaper, pink curtains, teddies everywhere! Definitely time to redecorate now that she was thirteen! She jumped out of bed wearing pink pyjamas and giggled as she looked in the mirror. Her long blonde hair was all - over the place as usual. She studied herself for a moment. She was not that tall for her age but she wasn't too short either. She had a soft look about her and a distinct oval shaped face with big blue eyes and long eyelashes.

She had always had vivid dreams ever since she could remember. Some things were the same; the pink coloured horse, the golden lion, the tiara; but some things were new, such as the castle in the mountains and the talking, yes the talking was definitely new.

It had been five years since she had first dreamed of the house and the dreams had become clearer over the years. She hadn't known at first if the house was even real but after dreaming about it for such a long time she had decided to talk it over with her family and that's when they had told her. They, Alice and Anthony, were not her real Mum and Dad, she was adopted. Her brother George was her adopted brother too, not her real brother. She had been eight years old at the time she found out but she hadn't cried, she hadn't even been upset. It was like she already knew and although she did know that they were not her real family, she still loved them very much. She still remembered how shocked they looked when they had asked her to draw the house in her dreams and she had drawn in such detail the house that they were now going to stay in for the summer. When she had finished the drawing they showed her a photograph. It was a photograph of the house. They said it had been given to them by the adoption agency along with Rose's most treasured possession, a beautiful tiara, set with small different coloured stones, eight in total. As soon as she had seen the photo she knew that she had been there before and she knew that she had to go there again if she had any chance of finding out what had happened to her real Mum and Dad. Now today was finally the day that they were heading off to the house for the first day of their holiday! She was so excited to see this house and actually feel what it was like to be there.

"Come on George, we'll be late" she cried as she ran from her room across the landing and banged on his bedroom door. "George, George come out! Oh where is he?" she sighed.

"I'm right here" George called from downstairs. He was full of excitement too and was beaming up at her. It was funny how they looked so alike even though he wasn't her real brother. He was two years younger but was now the same height and he had the same blue eyes, long eyelashes, gentle features and oval shaped face. They were both very good natured children and loved to spend time together around their family home in the English countryside. They had both grown up there and knew the area well. Rolling hills, rivers and streams surrounded their cottage and had enabled them to enjoy an idyllic upbringing in one of the most beautiful parts of England. Close by was their school, set squarely in the centre of the pretty village where Alice and Anthony both worked. In fact their parents were both born there and had lived there all of their lives. Truth be told none of them could imagine living anywhere else. It was just too beautiful.

The family cottage, was surrounded by countless flowers and gardens where they also grew their own vegetables. Just around the back through their main garden, past the children's slide, swings and treehouse were the orchards. Apples, plums, pears, cherries, you name it. There was always something tasty to try and Alice made the most delicious fruit crumbles.

Being in the heart of the country also meant that they were surrounded by animals and nature, horses, sheep, cows, ducks, birds and butterflies. Beautiful sounds of birds singing and trees swaying always filled the air.

Rose and George ran into the kitchen where their parents were sitting at the breakfast table eating their cornflakes. The children sat down and started tucking into their toast and marmite.

"So are you all packed and ready for the trip, my lovelies?" asked Alice with a smile. She was a beautiful lady and in stark contrast to the children she had red hair, just over her shoulders. She had a lovely warm smile and a kind face and the most gorgeous blue eyes that shone. There really weren't many people you could meet who were kinder and she spent most of her time taking care of her family and friends and pretty much anyone else who needed it!

"Of course they're packed" said Anthony finishing off his second cup of tea of the morning. Although he didn't have much hair left these days, this didn't take away the fact that he was still a handsome man and he also continued in the family tradition of kindness. "But we all had better hurry up or we'll be late."

They finished up their breakfast and rushed around the house, getting washed and dressed before jumping into the car, ready to hit the road.

The drive would take them a while and they spent most of the time looking out the window at all of the fields, trees and wildlife they passed, including a safari park where they caught a glimpse of the lions and zebras roaming around. Rose remembered going there a few years earlier and had always thought that working there with the animals and learning all about their wonderful ways would just be the best job in the world. She had always been drawn to animals and sometimes she thought that they were easier to get along with than people and that we could learn so much from how they behaved. Along the way Rose told her family that she had had another dream and that this time there had been a flying horse and a talking lion. By now they were all used to Rose's dreams and the general mood in the car was happy and excited as they covered the many miles of their journey. After a quick stop for lunch the time passed quickly and pretty soon they were heading to the Dorset coast towards the town of Weymouth where their adventure would begin.

As they pulled into the main entrance Rose and George looked at each other with big, wide grins. It was just as they had imagined, densely thick trees meeting in the middle of the road above them, making it seem as though they were heading into a dark tunnel. Looking into the distance they could see the house and a large open space in front of them. There were two other cars, belonging to their friends, already parked up outside the main house.

"How come we're always the last ones to arrive?" said Rose laughing as they pulled up next to the house. "They always seem to beat us somehow."

"I don't know darling but I expect the others are in the garden making the most of it on a beautiful day like this" said Alice, almost to herself as they all jumped out of the car and started unpacking their bags. That is, all except Rose who just stood there as still as a statue staring at the house.

"It's just wonderful" she said as she finally started to snap out of it "It's exactly how I knew it would be. Oh, I'm so excited, I just know that we are going to have the most amazing time here, I can just feel it." With that she picked up her bag and headed into the house with the others. After all now they were here it was time to go exploring with their friends.

Chapter 2 - The Discovery

The house was fantastic, it had nine bedrooms in total and was surrounded on all sides by tall trees with glimpses of sunlight peeking through and what's more, it was only a fifteen minute walk to the coastline. Inside, their friends were waiting for them. It was so good to see them all again and to know that they were going to be together for three whole weeks.

Callum was the first one to spot them as he came running in followed by the others. Callum was a very friendly lad, aged fourteen and lots of fun. As always he gave both Rose and George a big hug and he jumped up and down enthusiastically.

"Let me show you around" he beamed. He and his brother and sisters Alex, Violet and Ruby, were from a town in Kent where they lived with their Mum and Dad, Kel and Christophe. They were all coming in from outside where the children had been playing. Last to come in were Lucy and her daughter Issy who were also from Kent but as Callum always put it, they lived in the country part really. They had all been friends for life and were all very close.

Callum and Issy were the eldest of all of the children at fourteen. Callum was sensible and very intelligent, always trying to figure out how things worked and solve any problems that came up. He was acing his way through school and was likely to end up a Doctor of some description. He was always up for a laugh and was great fun. He wore trendy dark glasses over his brown eyes, which matched his thick brown hair and was quite a stocky lad, not particularly tall for his age. Issy on the other hand was very tall and slim and although she had just turned fourteen she was already taller than her mum! She had long brown hair and big blue eyes with a lovely kind face. She was very kind in her nature and always made sure everyone was alright and she knew how to stand up for herself too.

Callum's younger siblings all looked pretty

different to each other, even Alex and Ruby who were twins weren't identical. Alex at twelve was the eldest twin by three minutes and both he and Ruby had fair hair, almost blonde. While Alex had brown eyes like his older siblings, Ruby had bright blue eyes. Alex was quite a timid character and spent a lot of time playing by himself, whilst Ruby was very outgoing and had lots of friends that she was always playing with, which was exactly what she was doing right now.

Violet was the next eldest, she was eleven and had very dark features, thick black hair and dark brown eyes. Violet was very independent and her mind was very advanced for her age. The phrase 'wise beyond her years' was something the adults always said. She was quite tall for her age too.

They were all eager to explore this huge house and so they all ran off with Callum leading the way leaving the adults behind to talk about, well whatever it is adults talk about!

Every room was huge and there were so many

rooms and beds to choose from, it was just too exciting. On the top floor there were wooden beams high up in the ceiling and there was a roof window looking out onto the woods behind. Rose thought that it would be beautiful at night to look up at the stars and was thrilled to see that the bed directly under the window was still free.

"Is it ok if I have that bed?" asked Rose. Callum looked around at the other children and they all smiled. "What?" asked Rose.

"Well," Callum said "we were thinking that we should ask if we could camp out in the garden instead. It'll be really cool." Rose and George's faces lit up.

"What a great idea!" said George.

"Definitely a great idea. I love looking up at the stars" said Rose.

"We thought you'd love that idea" said Issy smiling even more. "Come on let's go and show them the grounds."

"We have probably got a couple of hours to go for a bit of exploring in the woods too before dinner." Callum shouted. They all agreed that sounded like a great plan and they ran downstairs and out of the back door into the garden that backed onto the woods.

"This is going to be such a cool holiday isn't it Rose" said George. Rose looked at her brother and looked back at the house. She definitely wanted to have a cool holiday but she also knew that this was a good chance for her to find out more about her parents. She knew that George wanted to help her with that too. But now was not the time to remind him, they would have a chance to find out as much as possible after the initial excitement had calmed down. For now she was just happy to be there with her friends and family. Instead she just said "Yes George, this is going to be a very cool holiday."

They were full of excitement as they walked into the thick woods. Rose walked a little slower than the others and was listening out for any wildlife. They were probably making too much noise for any of the animals to come close but she hoped they would spot something.

"I wonder what we'll find" said George.

"I hope we find treasure" shouted Alex.

"This is so exciting" Ruby cried.

After a while the pathway started to branch in different directions and they decided to walk away from the path and just go as deep as they could into the woods. That's where they found the cave.

At first they just stood there staring wondering if they should go inside.

"Who wants to go first?" Issy asked. They all looked around. Suddenly it seemed a bit different, maybe even a bit scary. What would they find in there?

"Oh come on you scaredy cats" laughed Issy. "This is England you know. There won't be anything scary. Let's go." Issy ran into the cave and the others followed, albeit with a bit less enthusiasm but once they were inside they realised they had nothing to worry about. The cave was large and spacious and surprisingly light as their eyes adjusted. Actually once they had been in there for about five minutes they were a bit bored and were ready to head back when suddenly Rose let out a cry.

"Guys, I think I've found something. Come and look." She was standing over a patch of earth that to the others looked just the same as the rest of the ground around it. "I can see something glowing under there. Look." The others looked at her and shrugged trying not to giggle. They were used to some of the stranger things that Rose came out with. They crouched down and started scraping the earth around it and before long they could see that there was something there after all. It was actually some kind of dark, sparkly crystal.

"Wow, it's amazing. It's beautiful, look at it sparkling" Violet gasped. "What is it do you think?"

"It's some kind of crystal and it's really heavy" Alex replied as he dug it out and lifted it up.

"I wonder where it came from" said Issy.

"I wonder if it has any special powers" said Callum.

"I wonder how long it's been here" said Ruby as they all excitedly talked over each other.

"I wonder if there's any more" George said suddenly. They all stopped talking, looked at each other and dropped to their knees, digging in the ground. One by one they started calling out as they found more and more crystals. All different colours and shapes, all beautiful in their own right.

They gathered them all up and counted eight in total. The large black one and seven smaller ones of all different colours. They decided to take one each. One was a deep red which they gave to Ruby. There was a blue-green one that went to Alex. A beautiful pink stone went to Rose. Callum took a greenish stone and a purplish stone appropriately went to Violet. George's one was dark purple and finally a dark blue stone went to Issy.

"I wonder what's making them glow like that"

said Rose. The others looked at her.

"What do you mean 'glowing'?" asked Issy.

"Can't you see them glowing?"

"No, they're not glowing Rose" Issy replied and they all giggled a bit this time, they couldn't help it, Rose had such a vivid imagination.

The thing is, they really were glowing. It was just that the others couldn't see it. Only Rose was able to see them coming alive. What she couldn't see was that on top of her head her tiara had also lit up. It shone so brightly but none of the others could see that either, nestled into her thick blonde hair. They had all fallen very quiet for a few minutes as they sat there examining the beautiful treasure that they had found. They all agreed that they would keep what they had discovered a secret from their parents for now and that they would hide the crystals once they got back to the house.

"We should hide the black crystal somewhere in the garden" Alex suggested. They all nodded and started walking back towards the house to clean themselves up ready for dinner.

Once back at the house it didn't take them long to clean up and they headed out into the garden for their first feast of the holiday. They had such a great time and ate their weight in jacket potatoes, burgers and marshmallows. Anthony decided to give them all a great history of the area and all of the adventures and activities they had in store for them. He explained that the woods were full of lovely animals and wildlife but that it was perfectly safe. They would spend lots of time exploring and that there were many interesting things all around the area and even some caves that they could explore. The children exchanged excited glances. Anthony continued by explaining that there had been many rumours over the years that the woods were magical and although that was an exciting thought, there had never been any evidence of this.

There was something in the way he said this that made Rose think twice. It was almost as though he did believe it was magical but didn't want them to know.

After Anthony had finished his story he told the children that they had a busy day planned tomorrow and to make sure that they got plenty of sleep that night.

"I know you guys will be excited to be sleeping out in the garden in your tents and sleeping bags but please be sensible and don't make too much noise" said Alice. The children all looked sheepish and they laughed. After they'd cleared everything away and got ready for bed they said goodnight to their parents and went outside and got into their sleeping bags. Rose was certain that none of the adults had seen them hiding the black crystal earlier. Did they know they had found them? No, that was silly, there was no way they could have known at all. It had been a long day and although they spent a few minutes talking among themselves and looking at their precious stones it wasn't long before they all fell asleep.

Now that would have been the end of it under normal circumstances; if this was just a normal wood that they had walked through; and if they had just found a normal cave with normal crystals. But the truth was it was not a normal wood, it was not a normal cave and the crystals they had found most certainly were not just any old crystals. In fact as the children lay there sleeping and the night moved on into the quietest hour, when the only sounds that could be heard were the rustling of the trees and the creatures scampering around who lived in them, something amazing started to happen. A soft glow started to appear from a corner of the garden. It was coming from the black crystal. It started off very small and barely noticeable at first but soon there could be no mistaking the light coming from it and it was growing bigger and bigger by the minute; until soon it covered the whole garden and engulfed all of the children in its soft white light.

One by one each of the crystals inside the children's sleeping bags started to glow and a light matching the colour of each crystal surrounded the children.

Gradually, inside each light the shape of different animals started to appear. First an eagle unmistakably appeared above Violet's sleeping bag, followed by a butterfly above Alex's. Next a dolphin was clearly visible above Ruby. A deer over Issy and a duck above Callum. Finally a dragon appeared above George and a horse above Rose. The animals were fully formed and were the same colour as the light from each of the crystals. The animals began to merge with each of the children, entwined into the beam of light from the black crystal and gradually the animals started floating one by one up into the sky inside the beam of light.

Around the garden the light faded and the children still appeared to be laying there sleeping but at the same time they were being carried off, each one of them inside a fantastic animal speeding up through a tunnel of light, heading into the unknown.

Chapter 3 - The Crystal Kingdom

The tunnel of light was magnificent! It glowed and pulsated in multi-coloured beams that surrounded the children, or rather, the animals as they travelled through at great speed. All of them were still sound asleep and had no idea of what was going on.

One by one, each of the animals sped off into a different branch of the tunnel until the only one left was Rose and soon hers came to a quick stop and she landed onto what seemed like pink grass in the bright sunshine.

After a few seconds Rose began to stir and before long she opened her eyes. It took a moment for everything to sink in and for her to realise that she wasn't in the garden anymore. She didn't know where she was but something weird was going on, everything felt different. She stood up and looked around. As far as she could see everything was sparkling and shining and looked as though it was made of crystals, shimmering in the morning light, a soft glow reflecting back from the grass and the trees and the land all about. What was this place and what was going on?

She could hear the sounds of birds singing and somewhere not far off water running as though there were a stream nearby. It was quite warm and sunny and although everything did seem a bit weird she didn't feel frightened, just curious. She stood there for a minute or two and then she started to realise that it wasn't just the world around her that wasn't the same, she was definitely different too. She looked down at her legs and they were different. They weren't her legs, they were the legs of a horse and they were pink! Was she a horse now, a pink horse? This couldn't be happening surely!

She started to run towards where she could hear the water coming from and straight away she could tell that she was running faster than she had ever been able to run before, in fact she was galloping and as she ran she was making a sound that was similar to thunder. The water was sounding really close now and she could see that she was coming up to it fast. As she got closer, she slowed down and walked up to the edge of the river. It was a crystal clear blue and was shimmering like no water she had ever seen before. But what was most surprising was the reflection looking back at her. There could be no mistaking it now, she had definitely somehow, turned into a rather majestic but rather pink horse! It was a good job she liked the colour pink.

It was at that moment that she realised that she was also not alone. Walking up to her were more horses, some of them pink, some of them golden and some of them white, each one shining brightly in the sunlight. It was too late to run, if that's what she planned to do, but she didn't have any plan of any kind so she just stood there and looked at them. They looked friendly and sure enough they stopped next to her and just looked back at her in return. Just as she thought her day couldn't be any stranger one of the horses stepped forward and of all things started to speak.

"Do not be alarmed. We will not hurt you. My name is Eden, please, tell us your name and what you are doing here".

"My name is Rose and quite honestly I don't know what I'm doing here. I went to sleep last night in my sleeping bag in the garden and now I'm here. Wherever here is. I really don't know what is happening." The horses looked at each other and started whispering among themselves before another asked,

"How did you get here?"

Rose looked at them all and started shaking her head and was about to say that she had no idea when she realised something.

"Oh. It must have been the crystals I found in the woods with my friends. They must have had some kind of power. When we found them I could see them glowing but the others couldn't see it. Somehow they must have brought me here."

The horses started to whisper among themselves but this time more excitedly before Eden spoke again.

"Rose, there is no doubt that the crystals you found were magical and what's more, you were meant to find them. The friends that you speak of will all be here somewhere too. We will help you to find them. Please come with us, there is much that we need to discuss and there is no time to spare." With that the horses turned and started to gallop away. Rose, realising that she had little choice started to follow them.

~~~~~

George had recovered from the immediate shock that he had somehow turned into a dragon, was in a strange crystal like world and could breathe fire and ice. He was actually quite excited now and was flying high up in the sky looking down at the new world around him.

There were mountains and lakes everywhere as far as his eyes could see some of them covered in fire and lava and some of them covered in ice and snow. This was the coolest place he had ever seen and he was ready to explore it all. He swooped down into a valley and landed next to a lake. It looked like it was on fire in certain places and he wondered how that could be possible.

"This is amazing!" He cried at the top of his voice and it echoed all around. The fire across the lake seemed to move as he carried on looking at it and suddenly he realised that it wasn't the lake that was on fire. It was some kind of creature laying on an island in the lake and this creature was breathing fire. George was wondering if the creature was friendly but he wasn't going to wait around to find out. He flew up into the sky and flapped his enormous wings as fast as he could. He looked back over his shoulder and to his shock he could now see that this creature was also a dragon, a much bigger dragon, dark purple in colour and what's more, it was following him. George wasn't sure what to do. There was no way he could outfly this creature, it was catching up to him fast. The only thing he could think of was that he would have to turn around and fight. He would have to take it by surprise if he had any chance but it was too late. The dragon had gained on him and was now right by his side. George closed his eyes and wished that he could be back in his sleeping bag, surely he was too young to die. He thought he was going to cry when suddenly he heard,

"I've not seen you around here before little dragon". Was he imagining things? George opened his eyes and the dragon smiled at him. "Where are you flying off to so fast? Don't tell me you're scared of me. I'm not going to hurt you. I just wondered who you were. I was about to ask you when you flew off so fast."

"Sorry" said George "I just didn't know if you were friendly or not. I've never seen a real dragon before."

"Oh, I see, so you are new around here! I knew I'd never seen you before. Let's go back down and have a little chat. I'd like to hear all about you and where you come from."

George decided that he could probably trust this dragon because if he was going to eat him he most likely would have done it by now.

"Okay, I'll follow you down" said George and

with that they both turned around and headed down to the ground with George wondering the whole time what exactly was going to happen next. When they reached the ground George and the dragon exchanged stories and as they both spoke, the other listened intently.

After a few minutes of conversation, George had found out quite a lot from this dragon. His name was Eldred, he was over five hundred years old and had spent his entire life living in this crystal world, which he had called Velaro Fore. George had also discovered that this land had been at war for some years now, ever since the King of the land Abner and his pregnant Queen Alva, had fled to escape the evil intentions of his younger brother Nerrez. None of them had been seen since as the Evil King had gone in pursuit of Abner and Alva and the only remaining royal figure in the land was Nerrez's Queen Maura, who had taken control of most of the Kingdom and its subjects. Those that remained loyal to Abner and Alva were not strong enough to overcome the Evil Queen Maura and Maura was not a strong enough influence on her own to overcome their loyalties. This had resulted in a stalemate, with both sides anxious and waiting for the return of their allies. In turn, when George had explained that he, his sister and their friends had found some crystals in the woods Eldred's ears pricked up and he asked George to tell him everything about it and when George mentioned that his sister often had vivid dreams including the latest one from last night of the flying pink horse Eldred let out a cry.

"George, from what you have told me, I believe that your sister and her friends are here somewhere inside Velaro Fore. We don't have time to figure out where they all are but for certain your sister will be with the horses in their kingdom. If we leave now we can make it by nightfall, there's no time to spare. On the way we will inform the other dragons and gather some support. If your sister Rose is who I think she is then we are going to need all the help we can get!"

George stared at Eldred as he flew off into the sky. He was so fast that George wondered how he would ever keep up. He took a deep breath and started off after him.

"Wait for me" he shouted as he flapped his wings as hard and as fast as he could. He couldn't work out at this stage whether Rose was in trouble or not. Were any of the others in trouble? Could they really all be here and if they were, where on earth were they?

They were indeed all there and to be precise they had all wondered the same thing, where were all of the others? As it turned out they had each had a similar experience, landing among their own kind of animal and having conversations with them explaining how they had come to be in this mystical land.

Violet, for one, had been flying for hours now as an eagle, heading towards the other animals that lived the closest, the butterfly kingdom; in the hope that one of the other children would be there. Thankfully, she would be in luck as Alex had landed in that part of The Crystal Kingdom although he was too bewildered to even speak and the other butterflies were unsure of what to make of him or how to help him.

Ruby on the other hand was having a wonderful

time. She had been transformed into a dolphin and had spent the entire time playing with other dolphins and learning new tricks. The dolphins told her that the best thing they could do is stay together and head towards the duck kingdom to see if any of her friends might be there. Which was exactly where Callum was, deep in conversation with the other ducks, trying to understand how any of the animals could have been taken over by the Evil Queen and what they might be able to do to help them.

Finally Issy found herself amongst a rather large herd of deer, all grazing together in the afternoon sunshine. She had taken everything in so far from what the other deer had told her and she was convinced that they were all going to end up in a lot of trouble. She spent a long time trying to persuade the leaders of the herd before finally convincing them that they must go and gather up all of the help that they could from any of the other animals who were nearby. Someone, somewhere must know what they needed to do in order to get back home.

Chapter 4 - The Crystal Towers

Rose had been following the horses for some time when she saw in the distance a magnificent kingdom towering up before her. There was a long winding pathway that led up to majestic gates that were guarded heavily by armoured horses. As she looked from side to side she could see that the walls stretched as far as the eye could see in both directions and that they spread out across a vast mountain range. Wherever they were taking her was a place that was very well guarded. As they galloped up to the gates the guards lowered their weapons and allowed them to pass through into the main castle grounds. They had slowed their pace now and all of the horses seemed to be looking at them as they made their way through towards the centre of the castle. Surely she must just be imagining things, why would they be staring at her?

"Eden, what is this place?" Rose asked.

"This is our home, The Central Palace. This is where our ancestors have ruled from since time began. Until things changed that is and our beloved King and Queen had to flee the land." Eden stood still for a moment as though she were lost in her thoughts then continued, "Until now I had almost given up hope that our land could once again be united but seeing you here means that there is still a chance that we can be victorious".

"What do you mean?" asked Rose.

"When we saw you earlier by the river we knew that you were not from this land that you were from somewhere else. We knew that you had come here through the actions of our beloved King and Queen. Somehow they have sent you to us and we must find out why. You and your friends must each have a role to play. We must try to find them before the Evil Queen discovers that you are here. If there is a message that you carry we will be able to find this from the Crystal Towers. It is not much further north from here. We must gather support as quickly as possible and then we shall set off." Eden started to call out to the crowd around them that they needed volunteers to go with them to the Crystal Tower and a number of the horses said that they would go with them and before long they had a large crowd of support.

"Rose, we are ready to go. Follow us to the Crystal Tower. Once we are there we will find out exactly why you have come here and where your friends are. Let's go." Eden turned to the other animals that were gathered around.

"We shall now go to the Crystal Tower. Call upon as many friends as you can, for our victory may soon be upon us".

With that Eden galloped off along with the volunteers from the crowd and once again Rose galloped after them, eager to find out what the Crystal Tower would be like and what it could possibly tell them about why she was in this land. Something told her that it wouldn't be long before she found out.

They stayed on the same road and galloped at the same pace for over an hour and Rose was really starting to feel weary at the pace when up in the distance they could see a group of animals standing on some rather large rocks. At first Rose couldn't make out what they were but as they started to get closer Rose could see that in front of them was a large group of lions and they were heading straight towards them. At first panic raced through her mind and body and she started to slow down her pace. There was no way that she was going to become the dinner for another animal and she ground to a complete stop. Noticing that Rose had stopped the other horses also stopped galloping and turned towards her.

"Do not be afraid Rose," said Eden. "The lions are our friends. They will not harm you or us under any circumstances. Stay close to us and we will go over and speak to their leader. He will no doubt decide to ride with us to the Crystal Tower once he sees you." The horses picked up their pace again and Rose followed them, a little bit slower than before and they gradually came closer to the lions.

As they approached them Rose could see just how magnificent they all looked and one in particular was almost luminous as it shone golden yellow in the sunlight. His mane was an immaculate circle around his head. His jaw was square and strong. The muscles in his body rippled as he moved. Rose was certain this was the leader of the magnificent pride of lions. Rose, still slightly nervous stood at the back as she watched Eden approach the golden lion and start to whisper something. She couldn't hear what was being said but it didn't take long before the lion called out to her.

"Rose, please step forward. Eden has spoken of you as being from another world and that you have come here through one of the hidden portal crystals laid down by our glorious King and Queen."

There was nowhere to hide as the other horses parted in front of Rose and so, swallowing hard, Rose stepped forward and approached the lion who told her that his name was Sunny.

Actually, Sunny was very friendly and Rose needn't have worried at all. He was excited to meet her and told her that based on the fact that she had come into their land there was a strong chance that the return of the King and Queen would happen sometime soon.

"We will ride with you and the horses Rose until you reach the Crystal Tower. Once we have received your message and the purpose of you being here becomes clear we will know what to do next."

"Then it is agreed," said Eden "you will ride with us. Let's continue our journey. We must find out what Rose is doing here and why King Abner has sent her to us."

If only they knew just how special Rose was at this point they would never have been able to contain their excitement. They had no idea at all just how important she was and that she had come to save them all. Rose of course, had no idea at this point either. She just thought they were going to be very disappointed that she didn't have any message or special powers and that once they realised this, then maybe they wouldn't help her find George and the others. That was of course, until they arrived at the Crystal Towers where they were all in for the biggest surprise of their lives!

The Crystal Towers were nothing like Rose had ever seen or could have imagined. First of all they were the most beautiful sight she had ever seen glowing brightly and changing colour every few seconds. They were also enormous and stretched high up into the sky further than her eyes could see. There were seven of them in total, wider than two houses at the bottom and as they stretched up they joined with the other towers and twisted around each other forming one gigantic column wider than a small town. Just in front of the middle column was a long staircase that led right up into the centre of the tower, where Rose could just about make out a doorway. Rose just stared at it in amazement while Eden and Sunny both stood in front of Rose and walked slowly towards the bottom of the staircase.

"Rose, you must walk up the steps of the Crystal Tower and enter the chamber at the top" said Eden. "Once you are inside you will receive a message of what to do next. This message will come directly from Abner and Alva. This will be the first message that we have heard from them for many years. No matter what the message is you must carry out the instructions and no matter how difficult the task, we will help you to complete it."

"What if there is no message?" asked Rose.

"There has to be" replied Sunny, "you would simply not be here if there was not a message. Go straight up the stairs now and into the chamber. We will all wait for you down here."

Rose looked up at the grand tower in front of her. There seemed to be little else that she could do other than follow their instructions. She started to walk slowly up the stairs. There was a kind of humming noise coming off of the tower. As she climbed up further it grew louder and louder and she stopped for a moment and looked down at the others. She had already gone more than halfway and she could see into the chamber. There was a faint glow coming from inside and she felt a tingling running through her body as she got nearer. Normally she would have put this down to excitement or fear but no, this was something else. It was almost like an electrical charge or some kind of power running through her body. Not far now and she would be inside. There was light pouring out and as she got to the last few steps this light seemed to lift her up and carry her inside. Yes it was definitely carrying her. There was no going back now even if she wanted to. She tried to stay focused on the light that surrounded her but it was too bright, she closed her eyes and waited for it to pass. The only thing was, it didn't pass and with her eyes firmly closed and light covering her completely she drifted off inside where everything gradually faded to darkness.

Chapter 5 - Princess Rose

Sunny, Eden and the other animals waited patiently at the foot of the Crystal Towers for a long time before they started to get a little concerned about what had happened to Rose.

"She's been in there a while Sunny" Eden said softly as she continued staring upwards, "do you think we should go up and check on her?" She watched Sunny's reaction closely to see if he had the same concerns that she did. She couldn't tell. She had known Sunny all of her life and he had always been very brave and strong, even when the Queen and King had fled the land Sunny had remained completely loyal and unshakeable in his belief that they would one day return. "Everything happens for a reason" he had said, "mark my words, they will return at exactly the right time. We just need to be patient." Their patience and loyalty had been stretched to the limit over the years. First of all having to endure many of their friends and family members from all of the different animal kingdoms give up hope and turn into vile, hideous creatures, followers of the Evil Queen Maura. Shadows of their former selves these animals now cowered in fear and anxiety to her ever growing hunger for dominance. Then as the enemy's numbers strengthened, they endured wave after wave of attack upon their home kingdoms as Maura tried to tighten her grip on her power. Every time she attacked, more and more turned to her side. If she could have destroyed them all she would have done it, but that had proved quite impossible. It looked at one point as though she may take them all over but somehow, she was not able to finish the job and gradually less and less of them were being turned, until not a single one turned, no matter how many times she attacked. This is how it remained. Although they were smaller in number, the remaining loyalists did not buckle under the pressure and had stayed strong in their stand against the Evil Queen. Eden was sure that this was in no small part due to Sunny and his unwavering faith in their rightful king and queen. She looked at him again, anxious for an answer, to hear his thoughts on their new visitor Rose and how she seemed to be faring inside the crystal chamber.

"Eden, look. Something is happening up there." Sunny spoke suddenly with excitement in his voice. It was as if he had known all along that all they needed to do was wait and it seemed he was right again as a bright subtle pink light poured out from the crystal chamber above. But what happened next seemed to take all of them by surprise, including Sunny.

Rose appeared at the entrance of the chamber surrounded by a radiant glow of soft pink light. She stood there for a few seconds and then suddenly she spread out the most magnificent pair of wings. She looked down at them and it was clear that in addition to those, she now had a rather prominent horn centred at the top of her head. She had been transformed again, this time into a beautiful Alicorn.

There was no need for Rose to walk back down the steps at all and she flew straight down towards them as all of the others gasped, landing in front of Eden and

Sunny she gently bowed her head and smiled.

"Welcome home Your Highness" exclaimed Sunny as he and Eden both bowed to Rose.

"Welcome home?" repeated Rose. "That's what you said in my dream! But I don't understand. I've never been here before. Why are you saying welcome home?"

"You may have never been here before" explained Sunny "but this is your home. You are the daughter of Abner and Alva and the rightful heir to the throne of Velaro Fore. They have guided you here to help us. Surely it can't be long now until they return. What message did they send you inside the chamber?"

"All I can remember is that when I went inside everything went black. I didn't know what was going on. Then as I started waking up I heard the words 'Go to the palace Rose. You must speak to Maura.' The next thing I knew I was standing again looking down at you."

Sunny looked intently at Eden who now spoke again.

"Rose, are you sure that's what you heard? We never go to the palace, we stay as far away from Maura as we possibly can. She has left us alone for years now. If we march upon her palace she will no doubt attack us again."

Rose looked at Eden and was about to speak when suddenly her horn began to glow. A beam of light shot straight out and covered Eden from top to bottom in a warm glow. A few seconds later she also had wings. One by one the light came from Rose onto each of the other horses until every one of them had been transformed into a Pegasus.

"What is happening?" Rose gasped as she looked at all of them lined up, completely transformed.

"This is part of your power Rose and part of your message," replied Sunny. "This is confirmation from Abner and Alva that you are indeed to head towards the palace and that we are all to come with you. We will go with you at first light, it is too late to head off now. We will all take shelter and rest here. Tomorrow, we will send messengers to each of our kingdoms to send reinforcements and then we will march upon the palace."

"Agreed," said Eden "we will wait until morning. There is nothing more that we can do tonight. Make sure you all rest up well, especially you Rose. Tomorrow is going to be a very challenging day for all of us."

With that they made their preparations for the night and settled down ready to sleep. Rose lay there staring up at the stars. This was all too much to take in. She had so wanted to find out more about her Mum and Dad and where they came from but now she was here, she still couldn't find them. Where were they and where was George and all of her friends?

It was just as she was pondering that very question that George and Eldred, along with another nineteen dragons that they had gathered together, arrived at the gates of the horse's kingdom.

"My brothers we have important news for your leader Eden, I am Eldred of the Dragon Kingdom" Eldred declared as he stood before the guards at the gate "please let us pass."

"Eldred, Eden is not here. She has ridden north to the Crystal Towers with a company of our fellow countrymen and a new arrival by the name of Rose. We are not sure when they are expected back but you are welcome to remain here and wait for them," replied the guard.

George looked at Eldred in dismay, "We've missed them. We have to go and find them straight away," he cried.

"I don't think that's the best idea George," said Eldred. "We will struggle to find them in the darkness of night and besides we have to rest up at some point. Let's spend the night here and we will fly out at first light and meet them at the Crystal Towers. You never know, they may even be on their way back here now."

George didn't like it but he knew that Eldred was right. He nodded first at Eldred and then at the guards. The guards in turn opened the gates and all of the dragons filed inside, led by George and Eldred. They gathered around the centre courtyard and settled down for the night. George couldn't help but wonder how they were going to find his sister and he hoped that she was ok. That was his last thought as he slowly drifted off to sleep.

Chapter 6 - Not Just a Dream

As the sun rose across the woods and into the children's garden, a golden haze filtered across the trees and brought a warm glow to the early morning. It was quiet and the rays of sun warmed up the tents as the children lay sleeping inside. One by one they started to open their eyes and stretch and yawn, shaking off the feeling of a very deep sleep. Rose was the first one to sit up and look around the tent. What an amazing dream she had had. It had seemed so real, so much had happened and in so much detail. Surely this house must have some link to her finding out exactly where her real parents were.

Today, she had decided that they would go back into the woods and see if there were any more crystals in the cave. Anything that would give her more clues to finding out about her parents. That was after they had been into town and down to the beach. One by one the other children woke up as they could hear Rose talking out loud. After chatting together they decided that they would get ready and have breakfast as fast as they could so that they could spend as long as possible at the beach before lunch.

It was a really beautiful day and they played for hours on the sandy beach running in and out of the sea, collecting shells and seaweed. They also had a wander around all of the lovely shops and bought themselves different sun hats and sunglasses. When it was time for lunch they headed back to the house and all sat down again together and talked about their plans for the rest of the holiday.

"As we're here for three weeks we thought we would spend the first week just relaxing and getting to know the local area" said Alice. "We can spend our mornings together down at the beach and about the town and you guys can spend the afternoons exploring the woods. In the evening's we can have a BBQ and play games together." Alice was always careful not to say barbecue, instead choosing to spell it as she believed that if she said that it would start raining and ruin it. "Then once we have settled in we can start exploring a little bit further afield and go on some walks and day trips and take picnics. How does that sound?"

The children all agreed that it sounded ideal to them and after they had finished their lunch they didn't waste a second before they were ready to head off again into the woods to see what they could find. Just as they were leaving Alice called out,

"Oh I forgot to mention that we have visitors coming over tomorrow around lunchtime, Mr & Mrs Johnson, who own this house. They want to pop in and say hello and make sure everything is ok for us. So tomorrow it might be an idea if we stay in the house until after lunch, that way we can all get to meet them."

"OK" the children responded collectively and headed off out the backdoor and back into the woods.

As they walked along the path Rose said,

"Guys, can we go back to the cave again today. I really want to have another look around and see if we can find any more crystals."

"Sure why not," said Issy "it was really cool finding them and there probably are loads more buried in there."

"Rose. When Mr and Mrs Johnson come tomorrow are you going to see if you can ask them anything about your Mum and Dad?" asked Callum as they walked together along the winding pathway into the woods.

"I'd really like to. You never know, they may have owned this place for a long time and they might even remember the photo. I brought it with me just in case. I was hoping too that we could go to some places in the town and ask around to see if anyone recognises them and maybe have some idea about what happened to them. If they're able to tell me anything about them it will be brilliant. I know so little."

"It's definitely worth a try" Callum continued,

"hopefully they will be able to tell you at least something."

"Let's hope so" said Rose as she wondered just what she would really learn about her parents from being around this house. "I had another dream last night and it seemed so real. I was in this whole other world that looked like it was made of crystals all around. I had turned into a horse, a pink horse actually and there were other horses talking to me. They took me to these enormous towers and on the way we met these lions. One of them was called Sunny and he was talking to me all about how their world had been at war…" by this point Callum had stopped walking and just stood there looking at Rose. The others had stopped too, they had all been listening to Rose telling them about her dream. George was the first to speak,

"You're not going to believe this but I had a dream just like that! I was in a crystal world too, but I was a dragon, not a horse. But the weird thing is, me and this other dragon, Eldred were looking for you. He told me that you were there and that you had become a horse!"

"I was going to say the same thing!" exclaimed Callum. "I dreamed that I was in a crystal world too and I was a duck. They told me that there had been a war and that loads of them had been turned into evil monsters and that the whole world was being ruled by an evil queen."

"Guys, do you know what this means?" said Issy. "I think we have all been in the same dream, because I was there too and I was a deer. Alex, did you have a dream like this too?"

"Yes I did. I was there. I was a tiny butterfly and I was really scared that one of the monsters was going to find me and eat me. It was more like a nightmare than a dream."

"What about you two?" asked Issy to Violet and Ruby, who both in turn confirmed that they too had a similar dream.

"I was an eagle," said Violet "I was flying

everywhere, it was amazing. At first I thought I was there on my own but the other eagles told me that it was likely that my friends would be there too. They said that we should fly to the nearest kingdom to us, the butterfly kingdom. Alex, that's where you are! Looks like I'll be with you soon so don't worry I'll be able to protect you. They said it would take us two days to reach you so just hang on." Violet smiled at her little brother and he smiled back. Alex definitely preferred the thought of Violet being with him rather than being on his own.

"I was a dolphin" said Ruby "it was just wonderful. We were playing and having so much fun. All of them were so friendly. In my dream we were going to swim to the duck kingdom. That's where you were in your dream Callum."

"Don't you see Ruby," cried Callum "this was not a dream. It must be real. There's no way we could all be having the same dream. What's going on guys?"

"I don't know." said Rose. "But it definitely must be something to do with the crystals we found in that cave. It kind of makes sense if you think about it. I told you at the time that I thought they were glowing, they must have some kind of magical power and when we fell asleep they took us into another world. Before we came to this house I dreamed of it years ago. Then the other day I was dreaming about talking lions and flying horses and now that's happened. In my dream the lion, Sunny told me that my parents were the King and Queen of the crystal kingdom, they called it Velaro Fore. He said that they had fled the land years ago to escape his evil brother and that they had left me a message so that I would be able to find my way home." Rose stopped for a second, thinking, looking down at the ground before suddenly looking back up again. "What if they somehow had come here? Maybe they somehow left the crystals here, knowing that one day I would come here and find them."

"Rose, this is freaking me out" said George suddenly. "Everything you're saying Eldred said to me too. He said that they had fled the land and no one had seen them since. What if they did come here? We could have just discovered something totally amazing!"

"Well what do we do now?" asked Callum.

They all looked at each other speechless. None of them could really think straight. So they just stood there all in complete shock. Their walk into the woods had just become an adventure beyond anything they could have ever imagined.

Chapter 7 - The Plan

After a while of standing there Issy finally said "What we need is a plan. When we go to sleep tonight if we end up in the crystal kingdom again we need to get together as quickly as we possibly can."

"I'm already very close to Rose," said George. "If I can meet up with her and the horses and lions we can all go together to the dark palace."

"That's a good idea," said Issy looking around at the others who all nodded in agreement. "I don't know how far I am from you guys but for some reason in my dream, I thought that we were going to end up in trouble and I persuaded the deer to gather up some support from the nearest animals. Those nearest to us just happened to be the elephants and rhinos. Now I know where you are I can tell them that we need to come to you. You need to wait for us to arrive, it's not a good idea for you to do this on your own."

"I agree," said Rose.

"Me too," said George.

"We already know that Violet is on her way to Alex and that Ruby is on her way to Callum" continued Issy. "If they can all get together and head over to the horse's kingdom we can all be together. At least that way we can be as strong as possible for however the evil queen will react."

"Yes and if we can find any other animals nearby to come with us then we will be even stronger," added Callum.

"So that's it then," said Rose "we have a plan. Everyone heads to me and until we are all there we wait. No matter what."

"No matter what" repeated Issy.

The children continued their walk into the woods and back to the cave. They spent hours looking around and digging inside and outside but this time they found nothing. As it started to get late they all agreed to head back to the house to get ready for dinner. All this talk of a war was making them more hungry than normal and there was a mixture of excitement and nerves among them as they ate and chatted to their parents about their afternoon in the woods. They all wanted to go back into the crystal kingdom but were secretly a little afraid of what was going to happen next.

When it was finally time to go to bed all of the children gathered in their tents and whispered to each other.

"Remember the plan everyone," said Issy.

"Everyone is coming to me and I'll wait for you at the horse's kingdom no matter what," whispered back Rose.

It didn't take long before all of the children had drifted off to sleep. The last one to fall asleep this time was Rose. No sooner had she closed her eyes than they flicked back open again.

It happened in such a flash that it took her by complete surprise. Sunny was calling out to her. "Rose, wake up. Quickly, we have to leave at once."

"What's happening?" said Rose, jumping up.

"Maura's spies have spotted us," said Eden. "We have to stop them before they reach her. If they let her know that they have seen you she will prepare her army at once. If we catch them that won't happen or at least if we keep up with them we can take her by surprise and she won't have chance"

"But I have to stay here and wait for the others," said Rose, panicking suddenly.

"Rose, your friends are days away. There is no way they will get here in time. We must act now. It is our only chance," said Sunny firmly. "If you want to talk to Maura you will only be able to do this if she doesn't have time to prepare her army. We will send word back and send for reinforcements but that is the best we can do. We must go now. The spies are getting away." With that, all of the lions and horses except for one turned and made after the spies that were just disappearing from view. Rose had no choice, she had to follow them and hope that she had made the right decision.

~~~~~

George had already been discussing with Eldred the plan that they had all made as they made their way to the crystal towers. It was going to be another two days before all of the others made it to the horse's kingdom and George was eager to meet up with Rose as soon as possible and was confident she would be heading back towards them already. So it was a bit of a shock when in the distance they saw one lone rider heading towards them.

As they got closer George called out "Where is Rose? Where are the others?"

"I'm Morgan. I have been sent back to gather reinforcements. Maura's spies were spotted by our watchman near our camp at first light. Sunny has taken everyone with him in pursuit. If they can catch the spies they will stop them reporting to Maura of Rose's presence here. They had to go after them. At the very least if they don't catch them they will be able to speak to Maura before she has a chance to assemble her armies."

"So much for the plan," groaned George. "Now what do we do?"

"I will go back to the kingdom as instructed," continued Morgan. "I will send for as many reinforcements as possible to follow behind Sunny as they march on the palace. With your speed you will catch them up quite quickly. You should send three of your dragons to get word to the nearby gorillas, bears and wolves. If they follow behind you even by a few hours Maura will know that to risk an attack without her full army assembled will be madness. There will be too many of us against her and she will have to agree to talk. She knows that none of us have turned to her for many years now. She awaits the return of Nerrez, her husband, just as eagerly as we await our beloved King and Queen. If she thinks there is a chance that Rose knows anything about where he is she will be keen to talk to her."

"That sounds very wise," said Eldred, dispatching three of his dragons immediately. "We will continue north and catch up with Rose, Sunny and Eden. If we get the opportunity to catch the spies we will wait as long as we can for you to arrive but we can't risk being close to the dark palace at nightfall. Something tells me that those spies are going to get word to Maura before we have a chance to stop them. In which case we will have to all head straight towards the palace without delay."

"May the spirit of Velaro Fore be with you Eldred," cried Morgan.

"And with you Morgan and with you. Come George, come my brothers we have no time to lose. Let us make good haste. Your sister Rose needs us."

Sunny stood watching as the spies got further and further out of sight. "It's no good we won't catch them now," he said. "We have no choice but to continue on to Maura's palace. By the time we get there she will know that you are here and she will no doubt be calculating a plan. Although I dare say she will be hoping that you will be able to tell her something about Nerrez. She has been anticipating his return for all this time."

"But I don't know anything about him," said Rose. "I've never even heard of him until I came here."

"Don't underestimate her Rose. You could know a lot more than you realise."

"I don't even know my own parents. All I know is that there is an old photo of my parents standing in front of the house that me and my family are staying in now for our summer holiday. I have dreamed about this house my whole life but I had never seen it before in real life until yesterday."

"Well Rose, I believe that your Mother and Father have been with you in your dreams this whole time. They have guided you here. Just believe in yourself and when the time is right your true power will take over. For now we have to continue on to the dark palace. Maura will no doubt be waiting for you."

Chapter 8 - The Dark Palace

Rose was about three miles from the dark palace now. They had been marching for most of the morning and it was heading towards the hottest part of the day. The palace loomed in front of her like a black cloud with lightning about to strike out of it. It had such a heavy energy and as they got closer they could all feel the negativity pouring from it. Rose was not looking forward to this at all. Her heart was thumping in her chest. She was glad that George had caught up with her and was very pleased to meet Eldred and the other dragons too. Having a few fire breathing dragons covering their backs relieved some, but not all of the tension.

At first it had seemed so strange to see George as a dragon but then as he said, it was strange for him to see her as a horse. Everything in this place was strange! Rose was also quite relieved to hear that the other dragons were bringing further reinforcements and that they, along with the horses would only be a few hours behind them and that this would be a strong deterrent for Maura even thinking of attacking them. This was something that Sunny and Eden had assured her.

Rose had no idea of what she was going to say to Maura and she hoped that something amazing would happen inside her. The others had said that when the time is right she will know what to do. All she could do was keep moving forward and when she was face to face with Maura just wait and see what would happen.

That moment was inching closer as they would soon be there and as they approached there were all sorts of ugly looking statues with deformed faces and bodies lined up along the path.

"I don't like the look of this place at all," said George eyeing each of the statues nervously, "and we're not even inside yet!"

"I know it's really giving me the creeps," said Rose.

As they got closer to the dark palace Sunny stopped suddenly and looked back at them. "Wait," he said. "Do you hear that?"

At first it was a faint drumming noise but within a few seconds it had got much louder and in the distance they could see a figure approaching them rapidly.

"Looks like Maura is sending us a welcome party," said Sunny intently. "Let's wait here and let them approach."

So they waited and watched as the figure became clearer and the drumming noise got louder until finally they could see that it was a large grey horse dappled with a long flowing mane. Perched on its back was a monkey who was beating a drum to a continuous rhythm.

The horse slowed from a canter to a trot when it came within speaking distance and eyed them suspiciously before he spoke. "Her excellency, Queen Maura has decided to grant you an audience. Consider her terms" and with that the monkey threw a small black crystal onto the ground which burst into life and projected the face of a very grey evil looking horse, her eyes glaring, staring directly at Rose.

"That's Maura," whispered Eden.

"I guessed that," replied Rose.

"So, I hear that you have come here from another world. How exciting! I bet you are having a wonderful time," started off Maura as she laughed sarcastically, the words almost spat through her gritted teeth. "Well since you are here we should get to know each other. Follow my messenger Krynto and I will grant you an audience. You never know, you might prove yourself useful to me somehow." Maura laughed her evil laugh and just as quickly as she had appeared she vanished again from sight. The crystal flew back up into the monkey's hand and the horse turned and galloped back off towards the palace.

"We must do as she says Rose," said Sunny. "If she wanted to fight she would have sent her General not her messenger. Besides, this is your message from King Abner and Queen Alva. You must trust their message.

Come on, let's go and get this over with."

So they continued their march straight up to the gates of the dark palace. It really was an awful place. Everything was black or grey and covered in spikes and shards of crystals that looked as though they hadn't sparkled for hundreds of years. There were bars and cages everywhere and behind all of them were snarling horrible looking versions of what once must have been friends and family of the animals they were with now. It was hard to make them out as everything was so grey but some looked like lions and some looked like horses. The atmosphere was so depressing and doom and gloom surrounded them.

"Maura keeps some of her worst followers locked up on display as a warning to all of the others. To stop any of them even considering trying to turn back to us. They take one look at these poor souls and they are scared out of their minds and just can't see a way out," said Sunny looking around in dismay as they started to cross a huge wooden drawbridge that lead to the castle gates. Underneath each side of the drawbridge the ground just seemed to disappear into nowhere, they were so far off the ground. It wasn't long before they went through a large doorway into the main section of the castle and at the end of a long corridor they came to another large gateway. Krypto snarled at them and said,

"Wait here," before disappearing through the gate and leaving them behind. A few moments later the gate swung open with a loud creak and they were greeted by a crowd of snarling animals, screaming and shouting and snapping at them and this time there were no bars holding them back. In front of them at the end of a long black carpet were a large number of steps leading up to a platform. On that platform were two black crystal thrones. One was empty and on the other sat the ugliest, greyest horse that Rose had ever seen.

"Silence," Maura screeched. "Approach, slowly." She dragged out the word slowly and laughed again, her laugh was more like a high pitched cackle which echoed all around the room. "No," Maura shouted, as they started to walk forwards. "Just the two of you." She pointed to Rose and George. "You two come forward to me. The rest of you, that's as far as you go."

Sunny nodded at Rose and George and as he took a step back, Rose and George started to slowly walk forwards along the pitch black carpet. They both stopped at the bottom of the steps unsure of what to do next.

"Come up, come up" Maura hissed.

Rose couldn't believe how ugly Maura was but that wasn't the worst part. The worst part was her smell. It was shocking and smelled like a cross between rotten eggs and the deepest dankest part of a sewer. At one point she thought she was going to throw up but she managed to get a grip and taking a deep breath she looked up at Maura and said, "My name is Rose and this is my brother George. I have come here because I have been sent a message by King Ab…"

"Do not speak that name here!" screamed Maura. "Never ever mention that name."

"I'm sssorry," stammered Rose, starting to shake. Her confidence wavering. "I have come here because I have a message. The message told me to come to you because I am looking for my mother and father and you may be able to help me find them."

"Help you!" said Maura sneering at Rose. "Why would I ever help you?" Suddenly her face changed slightly and it was clear that a thought had crossed her mind. She laughed again, this time more genuinely and looked at Rose with the most sincere face she could manage. "I'm sorry dear. We seem to have got off on the wrong foot. I will do my best to help you, if you also help me."

"Ok," said Rose hesitantly.

"Tell me everything you know about your parents."

Rose started to tell Maura about how she had been adopted and that she had a photo of a house that she had dreamed of and that her parents had left her with a tiara. She also told her about the crystals they found in the woods that had brought them there.

"I see," said Maura smiling. "Very interesting. It seems that your mother and father have wanted you to come to that house and to find the crystals. Very well. You have indeed helped me and now I shall help you. Your parents are most probably dead."

"No that's not true," shouted Rose.

"Don't you dare say that," said George, springing to Rose's defence.

"Believe what you want but they fled this land like cowards and it looks like they gave you up; knowing that they wouldn't survive for long in your world and that they were too weak to return here. My brave husband Nerrez, chased after them, risking his life to try and bring them back. He has been gone ever since and it's all their fault." She looked down, faking a cry with a pathetic whimper. "He's probably dead too. That's all I have to say on the matter. You must leave at once and do not ever come back here again or you will most certainly pay the price."

"Don't listen to her Rose, it's not true," said

George. "Come on let's go. We'll find them somehow. There must be another way."

Rose looked at Maura and then back at George. "You're right, let's get out of here."

They walked back to Sunny and the others and fled the dark palace, riding as fast as they could back to the horse's kingdom, making it just before nightfall. Rose's head was spinning and all she could think was that deep inside she knew that her parents were not dead. They were still leading her and guiding her somehow. She talked over their options with the others and decided that they would try to bring the crystals in with them next time they transported. Maybe if they had them with them it would give them a clue as to what to do next. They would also search deeper into the woods to see if they could find any trace of Abner and Alva. Hopefully, Issy, Callum, Alex, Ruby and Violet would arrive sometime tomorrow and then at least with all of them together they could make sure they all stayed safe and could work something out. There was nothing else they could do at this point and as Rose lay there ready to sleep she hoped that they could find something back in the woods that would lead her closer to finding her parents.

Back inside the dark palace Maura stood tall and proud in front of her hideous followers and shouted at the top of her voice "Yesssssss!! It is time! Nerrez will be back here soon. Those fools are no match for him. Prepare our full army, assemble all of the troops. We will be going to war again and this time none of them will be able to resist. This is the end of the crystal kingdom. The end for Velaro Fore!"

Chapter 9 - Mr & Mrs Johnson

When Rose opened her eyes and found herself back in the garden, she didn't waste any time in waking the others up. They gathered inside the girl's tent and Rose and George updated the others on what had happened and what they needed to do today.

Alex was the first to speak. "This is so bad," he said putting his hands to his face.

"What's wrong Alex," asked Callum, concerned about his little brother.

"Violet, you tell him," replied Alex, looking down at the ground, "I can't bear to say it."

"Oh dear, I just don't know where to start" began Violet. "I made it over to the butterfly kingdom to help Alex but it was too late. Alex had changed in some way. He was all deformed and had turned grey. It was horrible! The other butterflies had locked him inside a glass cage to quarantine him from them. They said that his fears had got the better of him and that he had turned into a monster. This is what had happened to so many of the other animals when Maura had attacked them before. They had got scared and given up hope. Once they were at that stage they were easy pickings and now because they were struck with fear it was easy for Maura to control them. It wasn't long from that point that they would start lashing out in anger. Seeing Alex like that was horrible. What can we do?"

"There has to be some way to turn him back" said Callum reassuring them all. "This isn't over, not yet."

"Not by a long shot," said Issy, joining in. "Don't worry Alex we will find a way to get you back to normal."

"This is not going well is it?" said Rose solemnly. "I'm really sorry I dragged you guys into this and it looks like it could be all for nothing anyway. Maura said that my mum and dad are dead and that I should give up looking for them."

"Rose you must not believe her and do not say that," said George, jumping into the conversation. "She's an evil liar and she probably just said that to try and stop you from finding them as she knows you're getting close."

"Oh I do hope so George," replied Rose, "I couldn't bear it if this was all for nothing."

"So let's stop moping around then guys and look at the positives" continued Issy. "Rose you mentioned that we may have a chance of finding out some more about your parents from Mr and Mrs Johnson when they come round later. You could ask them about what they looked like and if they have been heard of since. Also, George and Eldred are already with you along with the other dragons and are getting help to come from the wolves, bears and gorillas. Violet has made it to Alex and between her and the other eagles and butterflies they can make it over to you sometime tomorrow and they can even bring Alex with them. I'm sure there are other birds that they can gather support from too."

"Yes," cried Violet, "the Falcons have come with us and they have said they will stay with us wherever we go."

"Great," carried on Issy, "I know that we will arrive at the horse's kingdom sometime tomorrow too and," Issy continued looking proud of herself, "I've got backup too! Elephants and rhinos!"

"Whoa! That's brilliant" said George smiling broadly. "At least we'll be together and we can try and work out what we need to do."

"Well Ruby has already reached me in the duck kingdom along with the other dolphins" added Callum.

"Yes I got there not long before night time and we brought with us the whales, polar bears, penguins and turtles!"

"Wow! That's an army in itself" said Issy. "Do you think that you will be able to make it to the horse kingdom tomorrow too?"

"Yes, definitely. We have already discussed it and we will get there sometime tomorrow evening." replied Ruby.

Rose had been sat there listening to all of the updates and plans. She had been taking it all in but inside she felt uneasy. Everyone was still talking and getting excited about how they were all going to be together inside the crystal kingdom. She knew that she should be happy about this but she really was worried about what Maura had said. She had been sitting near the entrance of the tent and could see outside into the garden and up to the house. All of the adults were inside laughing and talking, although she couldn't hear what they were saying. It was another bright sunny morning and the garden was full of life. Bees were dancing from one flower to another and birds were chirping in the trees overhead. She looked back at the others who were all staring at her. "What?" she asked.

"Your hair just changed colour Rose" said

George. "It went pink for a few seconds and was glowing.

"That's crazy. It can't have been. Mind you with everything else that's going on that seems to be the least crazy thing. I wonder why it did that. It's never happened before. Well, at least I think it's never happened before."

Just as she said that there was a shout from the house across the garden.

"Children, are you up yet? It's nearly eleven O'clock" came the sound of Alice's voice. "Mr and Mrs Johnson are here. Go upstairs and get yourselves ready and then come back down and help us get lunch ready please."

The children jumped up and ran into the house and got themselves ready as quick as they could and then started helping out in the kitchen. Soon after they were all sitting down together to a lovely lunch of pizza and pasta. Although Issy didn't really like Pizza which she just described as 'cheese on bread and pointless', so she just had extra carbonara which was her favourite anyway.

Mr and Mrs Johnson were really nice. They were a sweet old couple really with silver hair and smiling faces. They told them all about the area and how they had been together for the last 14 years. Mr Johnson had met Mrs Johnson in the local community centre and she had been amazed that she had never bumped into him since they had both lived in the same town all of their lives.

"We bought this house straight away," explained Mrs Johnson "we just fell in love with it. Well actually you fell in love with it first didn't you darling. You were quite obsessed with it in fact. Eventually you convinced me that we should buy it and so we did." She smiled at her husband as he nodded enthusiastically and gazed back at her adoringly. "Then suddenly about eighteen months ago he said that he didn't feel as comfortable getting up and down the stairs and so we moved into a bungalow in town and started renting this house out to families for their holidays. We do hope you like it here."

"Oh we love it everyone don't we?" said Alice looking around. Everyone replied at once that it was lovely. "In fact young Rose here has been an admirer of this place for a long time too. She was desperate for us to come here for this holiday so that she could find out about her mum and dad. Rose, why don't you tell them about the photo?"

"Photo, what photo?" asked Mr Johnson suddenly. "Let me see it!"

"Darling, what's got into you?" said Mrs Johnson laughing nervously, blushing and slightly embarrassed by her husband's bluntness.

Rose sat there, frozen to the spot. Suddenly she couldn't speak. She had so much wanted to ask them all about the photo and about her mum and dad but she literally couldn't say a word. It was like she had been struck dumb. She looked around and opened and shut her mouth but no words came out. Not even a squeak. She could feel her heart beating faster.

"Go on Rose, tell them about the photo, about your dreams. This is your chance to try and find out about your mum and dad."

"Mum I don't think she wants to" interrupted George. "Maybe she's not feeling well.

"She looks ok. Well maybe it's better if you tell them instead George" said Alice, feeling slightly uncomfortable that her guests were looking at her with a "can't you control your children" expression all over their faces.

"No Mum, I don't think I can remember about it" said George pleadingly.

"This is outrageous" shouted Mr Johnson standing up suddenly.

"David, what are you doing" whispered Mrs Johnson out of the corner of her mouth. Staring at her husband in disbelief.

"I'm so sorry," said Mr Johnson catching himself suddenly, "It's just I wasn't feeling too well suddenly. I'll be alright. I just need to sit down for a moment."

A minute passed and no-one said a word. Then

outside there was a big clap of thunder, followed by flashes of lightning and a few seconds later the heavens opened up and rain poured down, hammering on the patio doors.

"Oh my goodness, where did that come from?" said Alice to the other adults in shock. "It was looking so lovely. Let me make everyone a cup of tea."

"I'll do it," said Lucy jumping up and she scurried around the kitchen getting everyone's drinks ready.

When they had all settled back down Alice turned to Mr Johnson and said "Mr Johnson, as you've lived here for such a long time why don't you tell us some stories about your time here. I'm sure the children would love to hear about it. That's if you're feeling up to it of course?

Mr Johnson smiled. He looked around the room at the adults and the children and then spoke very slowly.

"Yes. I've got a story for you" he began.

Chapter 10 - A Fateful Night

"Fourteen years ago I was walking up here in the woods with my old dog Toby, God rest his soul," Mr Johnson began. "It was the most beautiful evening. The sun was glowing softly through the trees and there was a gentle breeze blowing. I would describe it as the perfect evening but it didn't stay that way and that's why I remember it so well. It happened all of a sudden. The sky fell dark and a hard rainstorm came out of nowhere, just like the weather tonight. Of course I didn't have my coat, or an umbrella for that matter so I jogged along the path a little and found some shelter under a great big oak tree. You've probably seen that tree as it's not far from this house." Mr Johnson stopped for a moment and could see that everyone was wondering which tree he was talking about. He chuckled to himself and then continued.

"Well as I was standing there I saw two people in the distance, coming out of this house. It was a man and a woman, quite tall like, both young and good looking too but they were arguing, quite loudly. In fact loud enough for me to overhear some of it. I remember that she was crying and she was saying "What have we done? Why did we do it? This isn't right." The man said back to her "We had to do it. It was the only way that we could save her." I didn't know what he meant of course I can only guess what they were talking about. After that they got in the car and drove off. Now it was still raining so hard and looked like it wasn't going to stop for a while so I decided to take a chance and I ran over to the house and onto the front porch to get out of the rain completely. It really was the most awful night and since I'd already seen them leave I thought, well what's the harm in just waiting here for a while' I really didn't know what came over me at that point but after about twenty minutes with the rain still coming down hard I thought I would see if they had left the key under the mat and low and behold they had. So I let myself in to dry off for a bit."

Mrs Johnson gasped, "Dave, you've never told

me that before. I can't believe you." All of the children giggled and this spurred Mr Johnson on.

"I know, I know, I'm not proud of myself but no real harm was done. I sat in this very kitchen, made myself a cup of tea and looked around a little bit." Mrs Johnson shook her head. Clearly she was not impressed by this revelation but Mr Johnson seemed unfazed and carried on with his story. "That was when I noticed all of the papers on the kitchen work surface. They were adoption papers." As he spoke those words he was looking straight at Rose and it almost seemed to her that he was studying her face. She could feel her cheeks flushing and it seemed like he paused for ages.

"I realised at that point, that's what the couple had been arguing about. He had made her give up the baby and she hadn't wanted to. He said it was for the best but I'm not sure that it is ever really for the best." Mr Johnson sighed and took a deep breath. "I wonder whatever came of that young child." He paused again and looked at all of their faces in turn, then continued. "That's not all I found though. There was a short story that had been typed out and left on the kitchen table. Some kind of children's fantasy book all about the woods around here being magical and mystical and another world in another dimension full of magical creatures and crystals. I mean I really don't know how people make this stuff up!" Mr Johnson laughed again but it seemed a bit forced to Rose. There was something going on here that's for sure and it seemed that Mr Johnson had at least seen her mum and dad and that they had left some clues behind.

"What did you do with the book that you found Mr Johnson?" asked Rose.

"Oh I left it on the table. After all it wasn't mine was it. By the time I finished it the rain had passed and I thought I'd better be off before that young couple came back and found me sitting in their kitchen. So I got up and left. It's a shame what happened to them though as they never came back here after that night."

"What do you mean?" asked Rose.

"They were killed on the road that night about an

hour out of town. I saw it on the news the next day."

"Oh Dave, that's terrible. I never knew that. You mean to say for all these years we had been living in a young couples house who died and you didn't even tell me?" said Mrs Johnson, again looking shocked at her husband's lack of honesty.

"It never even occurred to me to tell you Jan. After it happened as you know, the house came on the market and we bought it and have owned it ever since."

"Well that's hardly a nice story to tell our guests is it? I mean especially the children and poor Rose who's come here looking for her parents" replied Mrs Johnson. "I'm sorry Rose, I really don't know what's got into my husband today.

"Oh I'm sorry if I upset anyone, I just thought you'd like to know about the house and the bit about the magic in the woods and that," said Mr Johnson sheepishly. Rose just nodded politely and looked at everyone as if to say 'now what'.

"What happened to all their stuff that was in the house?" asked George.

"Now that's a good question young man" said Mr Johnson. "It was empty when I came back to view it. I imagine the estate agents forwarded it all on to their family. It's a shame as I would have liked to have read that story again. It was talking about crystals being hidden somewhere around here. I must admit, I don't normally believe in those sort of things but it did make me wonder from time to time. Anyway, I think we should probably head off now that the rain has stopped" he said, getting up from his chair and bidding Mrs Johnson to do the same. "Thank you for the lunch and the cup of tea. We hope you enjoy the rest of your stay here."

"Thank you for coming over and checking on us. We'll be sure to let you know if there's anything we need. I'll see you out" said Alice also standing up and leading them to the door.

"Goodbye everyone," said Mr Johnson.

"Goodbye" said Mrs Johnson.

Everyone else waved and said goodbye and once they were out of the door the children asked straight away if they could be excused and when Alice said this was okay they ran upstairs to discuss what had just happened. Rose was sure that there was more to Mr Johnson than met the eye.

Chapter 11 - What Now?

"He knows something, I know he knows something!" started off Rose. "It was just really weird the way he kept looking at me when he was saying certain things like 'the girl was adopted' it was freaking me out, and when I went to speak at the beginning and couldn't talk I knew something was wrong."

"You mean you couldn't speak at all?" asked George "I just thought you didn't want to say anything!"

"No I couldn't say anything. Nothing was coming out. It was like something was stopping me."

"There's definitely something up with him then" said Issy. "It was like you were being warned in some way. Maybe you're just not supposed to tell too many people about what's going on."

"I don't know what it is," continued Rose "but it

doesn't matter anyway does it. He said as well that my parents are dead" she said sighing and looking at the others for help.

"You don't know that it's true Rose," said George, jumping in again. "Why don't we look on the internet and look for the news reports. There's bound to be something on there."

"Great idea" said Rose, pulling out her phone from her pocket as the others did the same.

They spent the next twenty minutes searching online to see what they could find but one by one they realised that they couldn't find anything. It was taking ages to get a signal anyway and every time they tried to look up different pages that could hold some clues they kept getting error and reload messages.

"Ugh, it's so annoying," said Callum after a while. "We'll have to wait until we go into town tomorrow. Why on earth hasn't this place got Wi-Fi?"

"Probably so that people actually enjoy their

holiday and don't spend all of their time on their phones and tablets" said Ruby as she realised at that moment her response wasn't exactly helping. "Sorry," she whispered and shrugged her shoulders as if to say, 'What now?'

Callum looked around and said,

"What about the estate agent that cleared out the house. I bet that if we go into town and ask them there's a chance that someone will remember what happened to everything. It will be worth asking at least."

They spent the next few hours going over all of the details of Mr Johnson's story. Everything from the couple being killed in a car crash that could have been Rose's mum and dad, through to the short story about the crystals hidden in the magical wood. They even spent some time writing a song about the Crystal Kingdom that mainly Rose and Issy worked on.

When they had finished Rose looked up at the skylight in the bedroom as the sun started to go down. It had been a long few days and her head was spinning. On the one hand she was thrilled to be part of such an exciting adventure and it had been wonderful discovering the Crystal Kingdom; but on the other hand she was feeling weighed down with the responsibility of finding the King and Queen and feeling that she was no further forward. Could they really be dead? Maybe they were but were still able to guide her somehow, she just didn't know.

There was a light pattering of rain on the windows and having taken off her tiara and laying it by her side she closed her eyes to let it all sink in, the others were still chatting excitedly in the background. She must have drifted off to sleep as she woke with a jump when Callum tapped her on the shoulder.

"Sorry Rose, I didn't mean to make you jump. The others have just gone downstairs for dinner. Come on let's go." Callum reached out his hand and helped pull Rose to her feet. He smiled at her and gave her a hug. "Everything's going to be ok. We'll work this out I promise."

Rose gave Callum a weak smile "I hope so," she

said as she followed him out of the bedroom and downstairs into the kitchen.

Everyone was rushing around getting everything ready for dinner. Although there had been lots going on Rose was still happy that they were all together on holiday. There was a large feast emerging on the kitchen table, lasagne, chicken kebabs, bread rolls, sausages, a huge Greek salad and a few other bits and bobs. The smell of all of that food was just amazing and for the time being it took Rose's mind off everything!

As they all sat down to dinner they all chatted and laughed and talked about everything that had happened so far and what their plans were for the next few days.

"All of us adults are going off early in the morning tomorrow," started Alice, "we've got quite a lot of boring stuff to do in the town. A bit of shopping and while we're down there we're going to have brunch in a nice little restaurant that we spotted. We'll be back just after lunch time. You guys are welcome to come with us but since you've been sleeping in so late we thought we'd give you the choice."

"I think we'll stay here. We'll be alright, won't we guys" said Rose looking round at the others who all nodded and mumbled with their mouths full.

"Ok, that's fine, we thought you'd say that anyway. If we're not back before you get up and you want to go out then please just leave a note for us and give us an idea of what time you'll be back," Alice continued.

"We will don't worry," said George. We've been doing a lot of exploring in the woods. It goes on for miles so we'll probably be doing that for most of the afternoon."

"Alright, well that's good then. That's what we were hoping you'd be doing. That's what this kind of holiday is for!" said Alice.

After dinner they helped clear everything away and then they all sat together and watched a film. It was one that none of them had seen before and they all loved it. After that they played some games which was also great fun. At one point Issy also played the piano and sang to them, she was really good at it and when all of them sang together it was really lovely. Rose and Issy at one point sang the song that they wrote and the other children joined in. It went something like this:

'Crystals shimmer, crystals shine, crystals sparkle all the time. Crystals gather peace to everyone they can see. They're like stars shining brightly in the big blue sky. Oh I want to be a magic crystal.'

'Magic Crystals take me by the hand and lead me to the crystal kingdom. Magic crystals help me understand all the places I can go and all the things I need to know to lead me home.'

Everyone seemed to love it. They spent the last hour before they went to bed sat out under the stars. It was so dark where they were that they could see everything really clearly. They even spotted a couple of shooting stars as well as some satellites high up in the sky moving across the darkness quite quickly and methodically.

When they finally decided to go to bed and were inside their tents and the adults were all back inside the children quickly recapped on their plan.

"We have to bring the crystals in with us," said Rose "and make sure we all meet up together at the horse's kingdom. I'll wait for you there and we'll come up with a plan. If we have the crystals with us that will help us I'm sure."

With that they all settled down and one by one they drifted off to sleep.

~~~~~

Inside a quaint little cottage about a three mile walk from the children's holiday house, Mr and Mrs Johnson were finishing off a cup of hot chocolate before they headed up to bed. As usual they both took it in turns to brush their teeth and wash their faces before changing into their night clothes and getting into bed. They both sat up and read for about half an hour before Mrs Johnson fell asleep and Mr Johnson reached across and turned out her reading light. He kissed her on the cheek and got out of bed for one last visit to the bathroom. Although this time, instead of getting back into bed he quietly tiptoed down the stairs and putting on his long dark coat and placing a heavy black bag over his shoulder, he slipped out of the back door and into the night, leaving the darkness of his cottage and Mrs Johnson asleep inside of it behind him for the last time.

He knew the way quite well as he had been there so many times and after an hour of walking at a steady pace he arrived at his destination. He slipped around the back of the house and into the garden and could see the children's tents pitched right in the middle.

He reached inside his bag and pulled out a large dark sparkly object which he placed on the ground beside him. After a few minutes it started to glow and with the soft light that came from it he could see through the tents and that each of the children had a small crystal in their hands. He looked around the garden and could see hidden in the corner behind a big rock another large dark sparkly object, almost identical to the one he had placed onto the ground.

He laughed quietly to himself and muttered out loud,

"All of this time!" He shook his head. "Never mind. I have them all now and this time there's nothing they can do about it!"

He quietly gathered up all of the crystals one by one. He knew that the children would not wake up from where they were even if he had disturbed them slightly. He knew that they were in a faraway land transformed into different animals. He was sure that when he had told his story earlier that they hadn't realised who he was. They knew that something was wrong for sure but not enough for them to know who he really was. As he stood there with all of the crystals in his hands he started to laugh a low and sinister kind of laugh. He closed his eyes and started to gradually change into his true form. He was fearsome, loathsome, ugly and dark. Another hideous beast that once must have resembled a majestic horse that was alas no more. It was also the end for Mr Johnson for he had completely disappeared and in his place was the evil king Nerrez. He was back and with a flash he shot up into the beam of light and back into the crystal kingdom.

The flash of light disappeared and the garden was once again dark, with only the moonlight shining on the tents.

Chapter 12 - Nerrez Returns

The children had all managed to arrive safely back at the horse's kingdom. It had been a good morning and it was great that they were all now together again, even if poor Alex wasn't quite himself! So far they had updated Sunny and Eden on everything that had happened yesterday at the house and had gone over Mr Johnson's story. Both Sunny and Eden agreed that it seemed as though Mr Johnson knew more than he was letting on and if they could do some further investigating then it may bring them close to finding the whereabouts of King Abner and Queen Alva.

They had spent several hours in the counsel hall in the centre of the horse's kingdom. It was an extremely ornate room since it had formerly been the very room in which the kings and queens throughout time had presided over matters relating to Velaro Fore. Now, their seats remained empty but all of the others were full. All of the heads of the other animal kingdoms had made the journey to be there and to discuss the very important matter at hand namely what to do next.

The city was now swarming with all kinds of animals from all of the different animal kingdoms. All of them ready to serve their rulers in whichever way they saw fit. There was an excitement in the air as they all gathered as close to the counsel hall as they could, hoping that they would hear just what was going on and what the plan was as the next session was about to begin.

"We now know that the children were not able to bring the crystals through with them despite their best efforts," started off Sunny. Although everyone had suspected this, it was the first time that day that this news had been confirmed and it didn't go down too well. In fact it caused quite a commotion as all of the animals spread this news around.

"How can we expect to find King Abner and Queen Alva without the crystals," shouted out Sterling the leader of the Gorillas.

"Order. Order. Stay calm please," called out Sunny. "It's just a setback, nothing more. The King and Queen will guide us in their own way and time, this I know for a certainty."

Everyone looked towards Sunny and as he was about to speak something completely unexpected happened. It felt at first like an earthquake had hit them, for everything started to shake more and more violently until Rose thought that the walls were going to cave in. Then suddenly a deep blackness set in, as though someone had somehow managed to turn off the sun with a switch. The shaking gradually started to subside but it remained there a little bit, just rumbling in the background.

Everyone froze. No one said a word. The children all looked at each other waiting for someone to say something, for someone to explain what was going on. They didn't need to wait for long for what had happened soon became very clear. Right in front of them in the middle of the room, just in front of the seats of Abner and Alva a thick black smoke started to swirl around and gradually started to take form. Before long everyone could clearly see, to their horror the full shapes of both Maura and Nerrez right in front of them.

"You fools actually thought that you were going to win didn't you," said Nerrez, sniggering with contempt. "Well I've got news for you. You have lost! Not only am I back but I am now more powerful than all of you put together. I have all of the crystals that these silly children left in the garden, including the portal crystal of the incompetent princess Rose. What can I say, like mother like daughter!"

Maura laughed at this and said,

"Thank you so much Rose for giving me the warning I needed to assemble the armies. That means that we will be ready to attack tonight. This time, mark my words, none of you will escape. It's over for you. This ends tonight!" She had such venom in her voice as she spoke the words.

"Sunny, your pathetic attempts to stand firm and await your king and queen have failed," continued Nerrez. "Tonight we will defeat you. Every last one of you. We will take the counsel hall. We will take the thrones that belong to us and we will take Velaro Fore!"

With that the smoke disappeared as quickly as it came and they were gone.

Sunny was the first to speak, "Brothers, sisters it appears that Nerrez has returned far earlier than we expected. He believes that he has the upper hand. However, I can assure you that he does not. He can never be stronger than all of us. He can never defeat us. We have the spirit of Abner and Alva with us right by our side in the form of their all-powerful daughter. Rose will guide us and tell us what to do and with her unlimited powers we shall prevail."

Everyone turned and looked at Rose and waited for her to speak. She had never felt so helpless. Surely Sunny couldn't be serious. There was no way she knew what to do. She went to open her mouth to tell them this and then something happened. She felt inside some kind of inner strength coming over her. Some kind of power, calmness and confidence. An inner knowing that everything would be alright. She looked around the room at all of the animal faces staring back at her and she all at once knew what to say.

"Sunny is right," began Rose. "There is no way that Nerrez can defeat us. If he thinks that we are just going to cower back and wait for him to march into this city and take it as his. He is sorely mistaken! We are the heirs of kings and queens, heroes and heroines of this land since time began. Our forefathers have been guardians of hope and justice for eons of time. We will rise up. We will remain united. We will prepare at once. We will march upon Nerrez and Maura and with the powers in us from our ancestors we will show them what we are really made of. Who is with me? Who is ready to take Velaro Fore back as our own?"

"I am," shouted George, looking at his sister with pride.

"Me too," shouted Issy.

One by one everyone joined in shouting their support for Rose and after a few minutes the crowd were all chanting as one.

"Velaro Fore. Velaro Fore. Velaro Fore," they cried.

"Let's prepare for battle," roared Sunny above all of the noise and the crowd erupted all starting to gather into their individual groups to prepare themselves for the march. "We will ride tonight!"

Chapter 13 - Preparing for Battle

Rose, George and the other children watched in awe as all of the various animals assembled themselves for battle. It was most exciting but also quite scary at the same time. The units were forming one by one in the kingdom courtyard. The gorillas were all lined up and were the first to be completely ready. As Rose scanned her eyes across she could see the elephants, rhinos, horses, zebras and lions. Beyond that were the dragons, wolves, bears and deer. Up on the walls of the kingdom grouped together were the eagles, falcons, jays, ducks and butterflies. Finally in the rivers that ran through the kingdom were the dolphins, whales, polar bears, penguins and turtles. It was an awesome sight and it filled them with confidence seeing how vast they were in number. There must have been well over one hundred thousand of them in total. Soon when they were all ready the children would join with them and they would march together to intercept Nerrez's army and hopefully catch him by surprise.

There were no weapons among them, they would fight hand to hand and defeat the enemy one by one. Rose really hoped that this would be enough. She had no idea where her confidence had come from earlier when she had rallied the troops. The words came out of nowhere and that feeling of strength and belief had filled up her entire body. It was gone now but not completely. She still had belief inside her but not to the same level that had come across earlier. She hoped that when the time was right that it would come again. She really wished that she knew what had happened to her parents. Was it really possible that they could be the king and queen? Whether they were her parents or not everyone in Velaro Fore could certainly do with their help and guidance right now. Sunny had maintained all along that they would come back when the time was right. Surely that time must be now. Nerrez had come back unexpectedly and they were now about to head into the biggest war this land had ever seen. Where were they?

The sky was still an eerie black although it was

only still the middle of the afternoon and the trembling all around still continued. There was a sense of tension in the air from all of the animals. They knew that this was going to be a formidable task and that they had to stay focused if they had any chance of winning.

"I suppose we should go and join our animal packs everyone," said Rose. "What do you think is going to happen?"

George looked around at the others and said "We are going to win Rose, don't worry. Sunny and Eden know what they are doing. They agree that this is our best chance to overcome Nerrez and Maura, to take them by surprise. Plus this is the message that came to you. You know that when you spoke earlier, that came from somewhere deeper than you. Sunny must be right. He said that when the time is right Abner and Alva will return. It looks like they will somehow join us. Come on let's do this every one!"

"Wait, what about Alex?" said Issy suddenly.

"We'll have to leave him here," said Callum. "I

hate to do that but I think this is the safest place for him. Besides, if we win then hopefully he will start to turn back to his normal self."

"Callum's right," said Ruby. "Alex will be safe here. We don't want him being taken captive by any of Maura's troops."

The others all nodded and then jumped up. They gathered together to give as close to a group hug that they possibly could. Then one by one they went and joined their animal units. Sunny and Eden were standing at the front of the assembled army.

"Brothers and sisters," Sunny began. "Today we are compelled to rise up against the evil of this land. We will rise up above fear and rid ourselves of their grip on us and our fallen comrades. Never before has the future of our world hung in the balance in this way. King Abner and Queen Alva have sent us their precious daughter Rose who we must protect at all costs. She brought with her brother and her dear friends. Due to their bravery and quick thinking they have all managed to come here together to help us and assemble our full armies. We can all be proud today to be able to stand up for what we believe in and to show Nerrez and Maura that we will never give in to fear. No matter what!"

The army erupted into a deafening roar that shook the ground beneath them even more and gradually, led by Sunny and Eden they were on the move, marching towards the dark palace once more. This time not just to talk but to take it back as their own.

Chapter 14 - Battle Formation

It wasn't long before they could see Nerrez's army in the distance. They had already come a long way and now it looked like they were destined to meet them head on instead of taking them by surprise. They were a formidable sight, twice the size of their army at least and Rose felt the early twinges of fear. Every single one of his horrible army were black, dark and dangerous. This was going to be a long battle and Rose just hoped that a miracle was going to be on their side.

There was probably only about another hour to go before they would be right on top of them and from that point on there would be no going back. George however, seemed to be completely unafraid and was flying right above her with Eldred by his side. Sunny also was completely focused and undeterred. In fact as Rose looked around at her friends, every single one of them had a look of determination that she had never seen in them before. She wished she felt as confident as all her friends looked.

They were approaching their enemy from higher ground which definitely would give them a good advantage. Directly behind them were the mountain ranges that the horse kingdom was so well protected by. To their left, much further down was a vast range of rivers and lakes that must have lead way out into the sea somewhere. To their right were more mountain ranges that led off towards the eagle kingdom and lands beyond that. Finally just in front of them lay the wasteland that led on towards the dark palace. It was a dark and twisted landscape that was scattered with burning columns of fire and sharp twisted figures made from the blackest, bleakest of stone.

They were about three quarters of the way down the mountainside when suddenly Sunny came to a halt. He turned around and shouted,

"This is as far as we go. We will wait for them to approach us and when I give the order we will attack in stages. We must try to divide them and when they come further forward we will send all of our fastest units around the back and try to surround them."

So they waited and watched and listened as the grey army in front of them grew larger and louder, every minute passing bringing them closer to their first wave of attack.

"Not long now," shouted Sunny. "Hold steady!"

"Hold steady," Eden cried.

They were metres away now and were running at them fast, heads down and snarling.

"Attack! Attack! Attack" screamed Sunny and with that they lurched forward en masse colliding with full impact into each other.

During the first wave of attack Nerrez's army were pushed back significantly. The Rhinos, elephants and Gorillas were perfect at charging forwards and knocking hordes of the dark troops out of the way with their amazing strength. The dragons were circling around above breathing streams of ice straight down onto Nerrez's troops freezing them to the spot and then the horses and zebras followed up, knocking them to one side and forcing the troops behind to gradually back off. George really loved icing the bad guys and was managing to attack more than any of the other dragons.

Sunny and Eden had managed to drive enough of their troops down and around the enemy on each side which meant they were able to attack them from three sides at once. They had also cleverly got the eagles and Falcons dropping rocks down onto the troops who had been frozen by the dragons which was also proving to be very effective, pushing Nerrez's troops further and further back.

Meanwhile across in the rivers, the allies were having a similar success rate. When it came to the water battle they had the advantage in terms of the numbers as there were far more who had remained loyal to Abner and Alva than had turned away and so they outnumbered the enemy at least three to one. They had used some of the whales to form a barrier across the river. The polar bears had lined up along the riverbanks and were reaching in, throwing the enemy back which had gradually caused them to tire out slow and down their efforts to get past them.

It took several hours but in each wave of attack Nerrez's troops grew weaker and weaker and it was easier and easier to push them back further and further until eventually Sunny and Eden had pulled all of their troops forward, down from the side of the mountain until they were all on the battlefield. Little did he know that that was what Nerrez had been waiting for as he demonstrated just how strong he had become now that he had all of the crystals in his possession.

It happened in a flash but suddenly half of Nerrez's army disappeared from in front of their eyes. Sunny looked around at Eden and Rose and called out with panic in his eyes for the first time,

"Something is wrong! Quickly, retreat back up the mountain," he shouted. But it was too late. Coming down the mountain at great speed were the troops that had just disappeared from in front of them. The tables had turned in an instant and they were now surrounded.

What happened next happened so fast that Rose barely had any time to even process it. Rose watched in horror as Nerrez appeared next to each of the children one by one and took them. Just like that. They just vanished. Then she heard Sunny shouting,

"Protect the princess, protect Rose!" as she saw him running towards her. In every direction she looked she saw animals running towards her but they were just being swept aside by some kind of invisible force. Rose looked across the battlefield and could see animals being overtaken by Nerrez's power. They were turning into monsters, they were giving into fear. She could see Maura laughing as she watched her husband outwit and outnumber them so suddenly and so easily.

She looked back around and could see Sunny getting closer and closer by the second when Nerrez appeared right next to her. She was frozen to the spot not knowing whether to run or to stand up and fight him. She heard Sunny scream,

"Run! Rose run. Now!" and she started to run. She could see beside her that those who hadn't turned evil were running too and they were running for their lives. A dragon swooped down next to her, trying to pick her up and was instantly struck by Nerrez and fell to the ground. Two more dragons swept down and managed to collect Sunny and Eden and move them from harm's way but for Rose it was not meant to be.

Nerrez used his crystal powers once more and opened up a portal right in front of Rose which she ran straight into and disappeared. Nerrez stood and yelled at the top of his voice,

"Victory! She is gone! She is banished from here!" He turned and started to gallop back towards the dark palace. "All of you follow me back to the palace now," he screamed. "I will deal with those others later. They are on borrowed time now! Maura, follow me back. Now! We must go back and celebrate my victory!" And with that,

Nerrez, Maura and all of the dark troops marched back to the dark palace having made the situation for Rose, Sunny, Eden and the children completely hopeless.

Chapter 15 - Trapped

Rose opened her eyes and sat up with a start. She was tense throughout her body and was sweating slightly on her forehead. She was back in the garden and knew that she was in trouble. They all were. Lying next to her were Ruby, Issy and Violet, all sound asleep. She tried to wake them up but it was no use. Wherever Nerrez had sent them, it certainly wasn't back here. She had to find out where they were and fast. She had to do something to fix this.

She jumped out of her sleeping bag and quickly poked her head inside the boy's tent. They were all sleeping and again she tried to wake them but they too were sound asleep. They were all tossing and turning and it gave Rose the impression that wherever they were they were definitely not happy right now.

She walked up to the back door of the house and

went inside, wondering how she was going to explain this to the adults. Everything inside was silent. There was no one in sight and then she remembered. They had all gone down to the town for the morning and wouldn't be coming back until after lunch. Sure enough there was a brief note on the kitchen work surface.

"Just reminding you that we've all gone into town this morning. We'll be back by three o'clock. Love Alice xx"

Rose looked up at the clock on the wall. Nine thirty am. She only had a few hours to fix this and at this point in time she had no clue as to how she was going to do that. The only things that she could think of doing was to call the estate agents in town as they had talked about yesterday and maybe she could get some kind of idea about where her parents might be. If she could find them then maybe they would know what to do to put this right. She went upstairs to find the notes they had made yesterday. They were in the bedroom under the skylight and right next to them was her tiara. She must have left it there yesterday when she had fallen asleep.

She ran back downstairs and started making phone calls to the local estate agents. Asking them each in turn if they had ever sold this house in the past and eventually she came up trumps. One of the agents said that they had indeed sold the house thirteen years ago to Mr and Mrs Johnson.

"Do you remember who sold it to them," asked Rose expectantly.

"Why yes dear, I do remember," said the lady on the phone. "I handled everything myself for the couple who used to live there. They were a lovely young couple and they were expecting their first child, so they told me anyway. They had bought the house in cash only the day before at an auction. They never even spent one night in the place. All they asked me to do was to take a photo of them in front of the house and then they handed me back the keys and told me to sell the house to the first person to come and look at it."

"What happened to them?" asked Rose.

"They got in their car and drove off and I never

saw them again," continued the lady on the phone.

"Was that the same couple who died in the car crash just outside of the town," asked Rose, her heart in her mouth.

"Car crash?" asked the lady. "They weren't killed in a car crash. They wrote to me about a year later telling me that they had had their baby girl but had decided to put her up for adoption and that I was to keep the proceeds of the house sale on account with a solicitor until they returned in the future to collect it. It's been thirteen years mind and I'm still waiting."

Rose was trying to process everything that was being said. It wasn't quite making sense. Mr Johnson had told her yesterday that the couple he bought the house from, most likely her parents, had died in a car crash. She decided to check one more time.

"I'm sorry, I didn't ask you your name," Rose said to the lady on the phone.

"My name is Isobel, Isobel Saunders."

"Mrs Saunders. Do you know anything about the couple who stayed in the house that were killed in the car crash?"

"Do you mean before the young couple?" asked Mrs Saunders.

"No, the ones who bought it from them, the couple who owned it after. There was another young couple who died in a car crash" replied Rose.

"I'm sorry dear but you are mistaken. There was no couple who bought it afterwards. Well not anyone who died anyway. The couple who bought it afterwards were Mr and Mrs Johnson."

"Are you sure?" asked Rose.

"Oh yes quite sure dear. You see Mrs Johnson is my sister. She bought it with her boyfriend at the time, Dave Johnson and they got married a year later."

Rose stared at the phone in disbelief. This was not what she was expecting at all. So Mr Johnson had lied to all of them, including his wife. Then again was Mrs Johnson in on it too? Or was her sister lying to her on the phone right now? It was a lot to take in and rather than risk giving anything away she just said,

"OK. Well erm, thanks for all of your help. I have to go now. Goodbye." and hung up the phone.

Right now she really didn't know who or what to believe. Her instinct told her that her parents were alive and if that were true then they may well be close by. Mrs Saunders has said that they were going to come back one day and collect the money from the house sale. There had been something very wrong in the way Mr Johnson had behaved yesterday and it seemed pretty clear to her now that he had been lying about her Mum and Dad. She needed to trust her instinct and right now it was telling her to go back into the woods and see if she could find another clue to her Mum and Dad's whereabouts or maybe she could find another way back into the crystal kingdom and do something to bring her friends back as well as her poor brother George.

Rose ran down the stairs and out through the backdoor and off into the woods. She would be very careful but she would spend the rest of the afternoon doing anything she could to find her way back to her friends or finding her parents.

~~~~~

Sunny and Eden had gathered all who had made it back to the horse's kingdom into the counsel hall and in the grounds outside. So far there were less than a thousand of them. They were almost all broken and hopeless. This absolutely had not gone according to plan.

"Sunny what do we do now," asked Eden almost in a whisper. Sunny looked at her and then looked around at the expectant crowd.

"I know it seems hopeless now," started off Sunny, "but I know deep down that this is not the end. It may seem that Nerrez has won this war once and for all and that it is only a matter of time before he comes back for us to finish the job but there must be a way that we can defeat him. What we must do right now is to all take a little time together and reflect. We will start a meditation together, we will all become still and focus on this moment. If we breathe together and reflect together the answer will come to us at the right time. This is how it has always been and this is how it will be once again. Let us do this now."

One by one they closed their eyes and reflected deeply, breathing in and out and quieting their minds to rise above any fear and doubt. They all knew that in the past the answers had always come for them and once again Sunny had given them hope that this would be the case again this time.

~~~~~

George, Callum, Issy, Violet and Ruby were trapped inside a large cage in the heart of the dark palace. Just behind the thrones in the centre of the palace were Maura's chambers and that is exactly where Nerrez had transported them to. Ruby was swimming around in a small pool inside of the cage while the others all sat slumped up against the bars. They could all see that

Maura was sat outside on her throne and knew that at any minute she would be back in there with them to taunt them again.

That is what Nerrez had said that they had been brought here for. For the amusement of his queen while he celebrated his victory. They didn't like it one bit but they were trapped. A couple of hours earlier they had thought that when they fell asleep they would go back into the garden like they normally did but without the crystals next to them this hadn't happened, as they had found out rather abruptly when Maura had come storming into the room earlier, waking them up with a rant that her husband Nerrez was taking all of the credit for himself for their victory.

On the other side of the room sat on a table was one of the large dark sparkly crystals that they could use to get back into the garden and sitting next to it were the different coloured crystals they had found in the cave. Nerrez had told them that he had put them there to tease them and to remind them that they were stuck there now as his prisoners. He had told them that most of the animals had decided to follow him and that the few who had escaped he would "deal with" soon enough. He also told them that he had banished Rose and that she would never be coming back. This had hit them all really hard. They all just sat there wondering what was going to happen to them once Maura got bored with them and where on earth was Rose and was there anything that she could do to rescue them.

Chapter 16 - Mrs Johnson

Jan Johnson took a deep breath and walked inside the branch of her local bank. There were a few customers and staff members buzzing around but none of them took any notice of her as she walked up to the counter and spoke to the cashier.

"I need to access a safety deposit box please," she asked in her politest voice. The cashier smiled at her.

"Can I take your name please?"

'Yes it's Jan Johnson. Mrs Johnson."

"Of course Mrs Johnson, please take a seat and I will get someone to come and assist you."

Mrs Johnson went and sat on a row of three cushioned chairs and waited. Earlier that morning she had woken up to find Mr Johnson gone. She had taken note of the date on the morning paper, 18th June 2017. It was something that she had been expecting to happen for the last thirteen years. All that time ago she had been sitting in the park on her lunch break eating her sandwiches when a very young and beautiful couple had approached her and sat alongside her on the same bench. Nothing unusual in that, but the conversation that followed had been very unusual indeed.

"Miss Saunders, we really need your help." were the first words they had said to her. She was confused at first, how did they know her name and how could she help them. They had gone on to explain that they were expecting their first daughter and had bought a house that morning at an auction and had decided to sell the house straight away through her sister Isobel's estate agency in the town.

They had told Isobel that they expected a man called Dave Johnson to buy the house from them and that he would come into the town that very day and say that he had always lived nearby but that this was not true. They also told her that he would come into the community centre this afternoon and approach Jan and would eventually ask her to marry him. She remembered laughing at this. At fifty nine years old the last thing she had expected was for someone to propose to her. Love at first sight was definitely not something she believed in.

The young couple had continued in their story and had asked her if she would help them. There was something in the way they acted that had seemed so pure, so truthful, so sincere that she knew that she had to help them and she promised them that when the time came, that's what she would do. They had offered her a large sum of money in return for her help but she had turned this down. She did everything they asked and everything they had told her came absolutely true. She had often wondered what had happened to them and if she would ever see them again. The last she had heard from them was when her sister had told her that she had received a letter from them telling her that they had had the baby. Maybe they would come back, maybe they wouldn't. Although right now it did look like it was possible that they would be back very soon.

That morning when her husband was gone had not been a shock to her. He was never really her husband. Oh for sure they both played their parts but she knew his agenda all along. He had thought that she hadn't known anything about him but she had known all along. That's why last night when he was lying about finding the house in the rainstorm and overhearing the couple arguing she had played dumb. She knew that this was one of the final steps in the part that she had to play and now she was finishing off the job.

After she had checked around the house, she had got herself ready and waited until after nine thirty as instructed and then had driven straight over to her sister's office.

"I've just come off the phone with a young girl," she had said. "She was asking about a young couple who had bought the house before you and Dave. Today's the day isn't it?"

"Yes 18th June 2017. He's gone already, he went in the night. Do you have my letter?"

"Yes of course, I've been waiting for you to arrive," Isobel handed her sister an envelope with the words written on the outside,

Do not open until 18th June 2017, on the outside.

They both looked at each other and Jan opened the envelope and they read the letter together,

Dear Jan and Isobel. Thank you so much for everything you have done for us. It will not be long now until we can return and thank you in person. Thirteen years ago we rented a safety deposit box in your name at the bank. It is box number eleven. There is a key for this inside this envelope. Inside the box are further instructions. Jan please go into the bank in town and open the box. We are forever in your debt. Love Adam and Anna.

Jan tapped the envelope and a small key fell out into her palm. Her mouth fell open.

That had been an hour ago and Jan now had been sat waiting at the bank for another five minutes. Presently a tall blonde lady in her early thirties came over and thrust out her hand. Mrs Johnson stood up.

"Mrs Johnson, I'm Rebecca Stevens. I'm the assistant manager," she said shaking her hand. "Please follow me and I'll take you to your safety deposit box."

Mrs Johnson followed her across the banking hall and downstairs into another smaller reception area with a large secure door in front of her.

"I need you to just sign in here please," said Rebecca as she pointed to a desk with a large book on top of it in which Mrs Johnson needed to fill in her name, address and signature, which she quickly did. The banker behind the desk smiled at her broadly,

"Please can we see your identification Mrs Johnson." he asked in a friendly manner and Mrs

Johnson showed him her passport. He looked at it for a few seconds and then pressed a buzzer and the large security door swung open. They went inside and waited for a few seconds for it to close.

"Ok Mrs Johnson I will wait here for you while you go in and access the box. You will see them all clearly marked with numbers and if you have any problems at all please call for me."

Mrs Johnson nodded and smiled. Rebecca pressed another code into a security pad and another door in front of her opened. Mrs Johnson stepped inside and stared at a wall covered in numbered boxes. She walked up to box number eleven and took the key from her pocket. Her hand was shaking slightly as she slid it into the lock. She turned the key and heard a click and the small door swung open. Inside was a small drawer which she pulled out and placed onto the table in front of her. Inside was another envelope a small velvet bag and a note which had written on it,

Dear Jan. Please give this envelope to Rose

this afternoon. By the time you reach her it will be around Three O' Clock. She will need the instructions that we are giving her along with what's inside the small bag. Please take a quick look and then place the bag carefully inside your handbag and leave the bank and close your account.

Mrs Johnson picked up the velvet bag. It was quite heavy considering it must only be small. She tipped it up gently into her hand and out slid a large multi coloured gemstone, all the colours of the rainbow but with the brilliance of a diamond. She gasped at its sheer beauty and then carefully placed it back inside the velvet bag.

With that, Mrs Johnson closed up the box and explained to Rebecca that she needed to close her account. This took about twenty minutes and she was now ready to head over to the house to give the news to Rose. Whatever this turned out to be, she was about to get an amazing surprise!

Chapter 17 - Another Transformation

Sunny slowly opened his eyes. Between him and the other animals they had been meditating for around two hours. It had worked perfectly and he now had a very clear idea of what needed to be done to try to rescue the situation. He looked across at Eden and then around at the rest of the animals. They had all opened their eyes and were nodding at him.

"We must go and check on Alex. He has a key part to play in this now," said Sunny, walking towards the door to the chamber where they had left Alex quarantined. He was still in there inside a small glass container with little holes in it. Still twisted and grey and ugly.

"Now Alex, I know you can hear me," started off Sunny. "I am going to call upon some of my friends to come and visit you. They will both teach you some lessons and if I am right about the message we have received, then you my friend have a very big part to play in how this will end." He turned to Eden and said, "Ask Nimith and Destiny to come as quickly as possible, we have some important work for them to do.

"I'll get them to come right away," said Eden, walking back out into the main chamber. She looked around the chamber and called over to Morgan.

"Please can you go and ask Nimith and Destiny to come in straight away. Sunny needs them."

"Yes of course I will go and get them right now," said Morgan and headed straight out of the chamber. It wasn't long before she came back with a Chameleon and a rather large spider on her back and presented them to Sunny and Eden.

"You know what to do," said Sunny to them both. They each nodded in turn at Sunny and then scurried into the room with Alex. "Now we wait," said Sunny to Eden as they both went back into their positions with the other animals, closed their eyes and continued their meditation.

~~~~~

Maura stormed back into her chambers, once again giving George and the others a start!

"How dare he treat me this way! How dare he" Maura spat the words out venomously into the air. "I've been waiting here getting everything ready for him for years now! And he comes back claiming all of the credit for himself!" Maura paced back and forth across the floor, looking up and down and seeming as though she may explode at any moment. George looked out at her and knew that he had to take a chance. The others froze.

"He shouldn't take you for granted like that," he said looking straight at her.

"What did you say to me?" screamed Maura straight back at him. George held his nerve.

"I said he shouldn't take you for granted like that. After all if you hadn't have had the army ready for him and been so clever as to anticipate his return I doubt he would have been able to defeat us."

Maura stared at him as though she wanted to squash him on the spot and then something seemed to take over her.

"Exactly! That's exactly what I mean! There's no way he could have done this without me."

"That's what I was saying to the others" continued George. "I said to them that Nerrez was lucky to have Maura. It was so clever of you to distract all of us by saying that Rose's parents had been killed."

"Yes, well, I didn't want you children poking around and finding out everything," said Maura, seeming to calm down a little. "Anyway, I haven't finished with you all yet. You may be of more use to me yet. I want you to tell me everything that has happened to your sister Rose. Everything that you can remember. Everything that has led you to this point in time."

George looked at the others and then looked back at Maura as she went over and sat down on her ornate chair.

"Well," he began, "it all started when Rose was very small."

~~~~~

Alice, Anthony, Kel, Christophe and Lucy pulled up outside the house. They had spent most of the day in the town and had had a lovely time. They looked around some of the shops and had a nice lunch right by the sea and were now looking forward to relaxing in the garden before getting everything ready for dinner that evening. They unpacked the car and went straight into the house.

"Guys we're back," she called out as they went through the hallway and into the kitchen. "No sign of the children yet." she said to the others as she started to unpack various items of food and drink from the bags.

"It's nearly three O'clock," said Lucy, "I expect they'll be back soon.

Outside from the woods Rose watched the adults chatting among themselves and unpacking the bags. She had seen them pull up outside the house and had waited another five minutes just going over once again in her mind what she was going to say to them. How was she going to explain what had happened?

She had spent virtually all day looking around the woods, digging and searching inside the cave for some clues and had come up with nothing. Not one single thing. She had gone deeper into the woods but she really didn't know where to start. It was just so vast. So it had come to this. She had decided to tell the adults all about the crystals and the amazing new world that they had discovered, that part she wasn't worried about. The fact that her brother and her friends were all trapped there with no way of knowing how to get them back was the real problem. She just didn't know what to do or say. She was just going to have to say it and hope that somehow the adults would have an idea that she hadn't yet thought of.

She started walking towards the house and

towards the door. Alice instinctively noticed that she was there and waved at her and walked towards the back door to open it. She must have been able to tell from the look on Rose's face because her smile suddenly faded and turned to a more worried look.

"Rose, what is it darling? Is something wrong?" she asked looking at Rose frantically.

Rose looked up at Alice. Her kind face was now looking very worried indeed. Rose looked out at the other children asleep in the garden and then back at Alice and stepped into the house. She opened her mouth to start talking when suddenly there was a loud knock at the door, followed by the doorbell ringing.

"Darling, sit down on the couch for a minute," said Alice, walking towards the front door. "I'll just go and see who that is." She disappeared into the hallway and came back a few moments later but this time she wasn't on her own.

"Rose. Mrs Johnson is here to see you."

"Yes Rose," said Mrs Johnson smiling, holding an envelope tightly in her hand. "I have a very important letter for you. It's from your Mum and Dad."

Chapter 18 - The Letter

Rose sat down on the sofa and took a deep breath. She had been staring at the envelope for several minutes now while Alice had been making Mrs Johnson a cup of tea. They now had sat with her and the other adults had settled down at the kitchen table just behind them. All of them wanted to know what the letter said.

On the outside of the envelope was written,

To Our Darling Rose. Do not open until 18th June 2017." That was today's date. Rose tore at the envelope and read the letter out loud.

Dear Rose,

This letter may come as a small shock to you so please make sure you are sitting down. We know that you will have been through so much and will have many questions. We will try to answer them for you in this letter. First of all we want to tell you that we love you so much and that no matter what anyone has told you, we are alive and well. When you were born we had to give you up for adoption to protect you and ever since that time we have been in hiding.

We know that Alice and Anthony have looked after you so well and that they will also have some questions that need answering. Rather than have you tell them everything we thought that we could answer some of the questions for you and them in this letter. Please understand that this is a lot to take in.

Rose, as she already knows, is not from this

world. She is from another dimension, a place that we call Velaro Fore, the children call it the Crystal Kingdom. We are from there too and if you had any doubt as to who we are, we are Rose's parents, Abner and Alva, rightful King and Queen of Velaro Fore. Before Rose was born our kingdom was one of peace but that all changed when we found out we were expecting Rose. My brother, Nerrez had ambitions for the throne and could not see past his jealously. This led to him and his wife, Maura turning away from peace and leading a revolution against us. We knew that Rose would be vulnerable to his attacks and attempts to turn her against us and so we fled from our home, bringing with us some very powerful crystals that would ensure that when the time was right and Rose had reached a certain age we would be able to return. We knew there was a chance that Nerrez would follow us through using his own portal crystal but that for him to do so he would be taking a huge risk. If he was not able to find us he would not be able to return as we retained the only two sets of crystals that enable us to transport back into Velaro Fore, along with a portal crystal that we have kept with us.

Again, we knew it would be a risk for us all to stay together so we took the hard decision to separate from Rose to ensure that all of the crystals were not held in the same place. Once Rose was born we gave her up to an adoption agency and left her with some important belongings, a photo of this house, a tiara and most importantly the eight crystals that we had set into the tiara. All along this has enabled us to keep a track of where Rose is and also for us to send her messages in her dreams, guiding her back to this very place."

Rose looked up at the others. They were all riveted to the spot and urged her to continue. Rose carried on reading.

The other seven crystals along with one of our own portal crystals we buried inside a cave out in the woods near this house. We knew that there was little to no chance of Nerrez finding these, even if he did choose to follow us through into this world. We also knew that when Rose reached the age of thirteen that she would be able to find them using her tiara and that we would be able to guide her here to find them.

We know that in the end, Nerrez took the risk and decided to follow us by using his portal crystal to come into this dimension not long after we gave Rose up for adoption. We kept track of him and figured out a way, using the help of our dear friend Jan Saunders, who you know as Mrs Johnson, to know exactly where he would be. Although he thinks that he has the upper hand there is one thing that he has not factored in, which we will tell you in a moment.

When you all came to stay at this house, on the very first day Rose and the other children went off exploring in the woods. They found the seven crystals and the portal crystal buried in a cave. They brought them back here into their sleeping bags and at night when they fell asleep they were transported into Velaro Fore. At first they thought this was a dream as they were living in this other dimension as magical animals but before long they realised that it was very real and although it was very exciting for them, there was also something very important that they had to do. They had to figure out a way to save Velaro Fore.

Last night things took a turn for the worse after Nerrez managed to find his way back to Velaro Fore using the crystals the children had found in the woods. He did this by sneaking into your garden. For all of these years he has been disguising himself as Mr Johnson, living nearby with Mrs Johnson,

waiting for his moment to pounce when Rose returned.
He didn't know for sure that this would happen but
he took a chance and stayed close by waiting for an
opportunity. As we said earlier he thinks he has
control.

The vast majority of our subjects have given up
hope and have turned themselves over to his power.
Only a few of our loyal subjects remain. The other
children, including your brother George have been
captured by Nerrez and are now in the dark palace.
They are trapped there for now, until they can be
rescued. Please be assured that they are quite safe, he
will not harm them. However, there is no way that
they can return here until they receive a sign of hope.
This sign of hope must come to Rose first then she

will take it to them.

      This is what you must do Rose. Mrs Johnson has something very important to give to you that we left for you thirteen years ago. It is a precious stone that we call the Rainbow Crystal. In your tiara you will see that there are eight stones. One of them is slightly larger than the others. This one is not a real crystal. It is in fact a piece of glass. If you push it hard it will fall out. Please do this now.

      Rose ran up the stairs to get her tiara and brought it back down ready to follow the instructions her parents had given her. She located the stone that was slightly bigger than the others and pushed it hard with her fingers. Sure enough it came loose and popped out. She placed it on the table in front of her.

Mrs Johnson reached into her purse and pulled out the small velvet bag and handed it over to Rose who looked inside and saw for the first time the Rainbow Crystal. It was absolutely stunning and she carefully took it out of the bag and pressed it into the open slot on her tiara. The whole thing started to glow round the edge of the crystal, where it met the metal of the tiara. There was a loud click and then the light began to fade. The Rainbow Crystal was now solidly fixed into the tiara.

Rose looked around at everyone who just stared back at her in silence and so Rose continued reading the rest of the letter.

Now that you have the Rainbow Crystal in your tiara you must return to the same place that you found the crystals in the cave. You must go alone. All of the others must remain here until you return. When you arrive at the cave you must wait for a sign of hope. It is very important that you remain there until this time. Once you have a sign of hope you will be ready to come and find us. When that moment arrives you will know what to do.

Be strong Rose. Do not give up hope. We will be together again with you very soon. Remember, we love you very much. In the end, love is the only way.

Your father and mother, your King and Queen,

Abner and Alva.

Rose put down the letter, looked around at everyone and burst into tears.

Chapter 19 - Change is Within

Destiny had spun an enormous web that extended from one side of the room to the other with the centre right opposite where Alex sat in his glass container rocking backwards and forwards with more and more intensity.

Nimith had climbed right up onto the table and placed herself into position just in front of Alex. The larger the web had grown the more Alex had rocked back and forth looking around with wild eyes as Nimith had changed colour constantly from her natural colour to the dark grey colour that Alex now bore.

They had been doing this for several hours now and there was no sign that anything was changing in Alex. That was until the chanting began. Nimith had started it off with a low hum and Destiny had joined in at a slightly higher pitch. Alex suddenly stopped rocking and started shaking instead, his wings flapping at the same pace as the chant.

"You are the master of your own fate" chanted Destiny as she span the web faster and faster.

"Change is within you" chanted Nimith changing colour more furiously.

Bright light poured out from Alex until it engulfed the room and for a few seconds nothing could be seen and then everything went dim. The chanting stopped and for the first time in nearly a week Alex was back to how he should be inside Velaro Fore. He was once again a beautiful butterfly.

"What happened" Alex asked straight away, staring at the large spider and Chameleon grinning at him broadly.

"We shall let Sunny tell you Alex" said Nimith nodding towards Destiny who quickly released Alex from his quarantine before beckoning him to follow them into the main chamber where the others were waiting.

There was a calm around the inner chamber as the three of them entered and straight away a smile came to Sunny's lips when he saw that Alex was no longer caught in the grip of Nerrez and Maura's fear.

"Alex, it is good to see you again" called out Sunny from across the room. "I expect you would like to know just what's been happening to you. Come over here and Eden and I will tell you everything."

Alex flew over and landed just in front of Sunny and Eden. He perched himself right next to the thrones in the centre of the room and listened very carefully as Sunny and Eden told him everything that had happened and what he must do next.

~~~~~

Rose sat next to Alice holding a tissue to her eyes. She had been crying for a long time now and she wasn't sure whether it was relief, shock, fear, anticipation or a combination of them all. Alice had been reading through the letter herself several times and had discussed all of the elements with Rose, Mrs Johnson and the other adults. The fact that none of them had passed out on the floor was a good starting point as far as Rose was concerned. It must have been as much of a shock for all of them to hear what was going on as it was for her.

The letter had clearly said that Rose was to go on her own to the cave where they had found the crystals and wait for a sign of hope, which was all very well, but none of them knew what that meant and what to look for. Having found out that the other children were trapped inside another dimension, Alice and the other adults were not keen for Rose to go out into the woods alone, to say the least. However, she was pretty sure that in the end they would let her and that this was what she needed to do.

It had been such a relief for Rose to know that her parents, Abner and Alva were going to return soon. Maybe that was where they planned to meet her. In the woods near the cave. That would make perfect sense, but so far not much else had made any sense and this had left her feeling very confused. There was not much more that she could do and having gradually calmed down she once again managed to find her voice.

"I'm going to do what the letter says" Rose said standing up and walking over to Alice. "I'm going to go into the woods and wait by the cave for them to come."

"I'm still really not sure about this Rose" said Alice, looking down at her with concern.

"Don't worry, I'll be fine. I've made up my mind. I have to do as they say so that we have a chance to rescue the others. There's no other way that I can think of."

Alice looked at the other adults and then looked at Anthony who nodded with his approval.

"Ok then Rose, you go and wait for them but I want you back before dark. Promise me" said Alice.

"Ok. I promise."

"Rose, please be careful."

"I will," and with that Rose put on her tiara,

thanked Mrs Johnson and went out through the back door and into the woods. When she got to the cave she sat down on the grass and waited, wondering just what might happen next.

~~~~~

Maura had been asleep for about an hour when George decided that it was safe to open his eyes properly and whisper quietly to the others.

"Guys, are you awake?" he asked as quietly as he could.

One by one they all replied that they were awake.

"What shall we do now?" asked Callum.

"Well, I'm not sure if any of us can do much while we're stuck in here" said Issy.

"At least we know now that Maura is not at all happy with Nerrez" said George. "I know it was risky talking to her but I think she believes now that we will take her side and to be honest, that might be enough to keep us all alive, if she finds us to be good company."

"I don't trust her at all" said Violet. "There's no way I'm going to take her side.

"I don't trust her either" said George. "Just to be clear I only started talking to her to buy us some time and in the hope that she would let something slip that would help us get out of here."

"I'm not sure that worked George" said Ruby. "I know you tried your best but I don't think she gave anything away."

"I know" replied George. "She didn't give anything useful away really. Other than the fact that she isn't happy with Nerrez. Maybe if I work on that angle more tomorrow we may get somewhere."

All of them were so deep in thought about how to get something useful from Maura that they didn't notice that they had another visitor. He had arrived so quietly and he was so small that none of them noticed as he slipped in through the window at the very top of

Maura's chamber and got himself up very close to the point where he could hear what they were saying.

"If only we could get to those crystals" said George, looking longingly. It was at this moment that their little visitor suddenly caught his eye. He was so taken aback that he let out a cry which immediately woke up Maura who sat up and looked straight at George.

"What is it now" she spat.

"Nothing, I must have been dreaming that's all" said George quickly. "I think I was dreaming of how unfair Nerrez has been to you and it made me angry and I shouted out."

"Angry eh?" said Maura. "There's hope for you yet boy. At least I know you are going to choose the right side. Now get back to sleep." She turned in her chair and closed her eyes again.

A few minutes later when he was sure that she had drifted back off George whispered "Hello. Hello. Maura? Phew, she's gone back to sleep." George looked around the room again and this time he was much more careful and didn't let out a sound. There right on the table was Alex. He was back to being a butterfly somehow and had come all the way from the horse's kingdom.

"Guys, Alex is over there on the table next to the crystals. So much has happened that I almost forgot about him. Somehow Sunny and Eden must have figured out how to turn him back from being under Maura's evil clutches."

The others watched Alex from across the room. Suddenly they had a chance. Alex had come to save them. But how was he going to do it.

Alex looked across at the others and then flapped his wings and positioned himself just above the portal crystal that was on the table and after a few seconds it started to glow. Then slowly a beam of light appeared from the top of the crystal and Alex flew into it, instantly disappearing out of sight. The others watched as the light faded and once the crystal had stopped glowing they all just looked at each other.

"Now what?" ask Callum.

"Now we wait" replied George. "He'll be back I'm sure. Let's get some sleep while we have the chance."

Chapter 20 - A Sign of Hope

Rose had been sitting by the cave on her own for several hours now. The tears had come and gone several times. She just didn't know what to do or what to look for.

The woods were so peaceful and the light that shone through the trees made beautiful changing patterns that danced across the ground as though it were part of a graceful symphony. There was the occasional sound of birds singing in the trees above and rustling of the bushes and leaves as squirrels scampered around her. A couple of times a deer had walked close by and stopped to stare at Rose before moving on in its search for food.

Normally this would have brought Rose peace but she knew that she wasn't able to find peace right now. Not while she knew that her friends were stuck inside Nerrez's clutches. She closed her eyes and lay back in the grass facing up to the sky. It wouldn't be long until the sun started to go down and she would have to leave to get back to the house. There was no way she could stay out in the woods after dark. There wasn't much time left. Maybe she should just do one more search of the caves.

She sat up and noticed that a butterfly had landed on her foot. It was a beautiful, radiant, multi-coloured butterfly that seemed to glow as the light hit its wings. She sat watching it for a few seconds and then realised that it wasn't the light that was making the butterfly glow. It flew off her foot and hovered in front of her eyes for a few seconds and then flew to about three feet away and landed on the ground. Suddenly a soft beam shot out of the front of her tiara from the Rainbow Crystal and covered the butterfly in its radiant light. At first nothing happened but then gradually the butterfly started to grow and change and before long Rose realised that it was Alex. He had somehow managed to come back and wow was she pleased to see him!

"Oh Alex, Alex you made it back. You're alright!" said Rose as she hugged him and kissed him on the cheek. "What happened to you?"

"Well, I managed to escape through Maura's portal crystal" began Alex. "I had to leave the others behind, I had no choice. They're ok though. None of them have turned bad. Maura and Nerrez have them locked up in a large cage but none of them are hurt. Oh Rose it was so weird. As you know I had been trapped almost since day one inside the crystal kingdom and I was so scared, but Sunny seemed to know exactly what to do and he sent a spider and a chameleon to come and save me. After watching them for hours I realised that there was nothing to be afraid of. Nothing bad had happened to me I was just worried about what might happen. I could see clearly that what happens to us is all in our mind in a way. I am the one who gets to decide what happens to me and as soon as I realised that I was free! Sunny told me everything that had happened and then he sent me to Maura and Nerrez's palace to see if I could help. This time I didn't hesitate, I just flew straight to the dark palace and the crystals were sitting right there in Maura's chamber. Oh Rose it's so good to see you and to be back here. What do we do now?"

"What do we do now? Oh no Alex, I'm so pleased to see you but I thought you were going to tell me. Seeing you gave me hope and now..." Rose's words tailed off and she looked straight at Alex. "A sign of hope".

"What do you mean a sign of hope?" asked Alex.

"I was told by Abner and Alva in a letter to come here and to wait for a sign of hope. You, Alex, are the sign of hope. Oh Alex, they are coming. They are coming here. I can feel it." Rose hugged Alex again and stepped back and as she did so her whole body started to glow. It was a soft pink that took over her whole body and transformed her back into the beautiful pink alicorn she had been inside the crystal kingdom.

"Jump on Alex" she cried. "We have to go and find the true King and Queen of Velaro Fore"

Alex jumped on her back and instantly she rode off deep into the woods. Faster and faster she rode until everything around her was a blur. They passed trees and rivers hillsides and valleys until suddenly they came to a large stream with stone steps across it and Rose immediately slowed down.

Right in front of them were two magnificent horses and they were walking towards them. The stream flowed strongly underneath them and Alex jumped down, the water reaching up to his knees. The sun had almost gone down and everything looked magical and calm in the glow of the twilight.

Rose bowed her head as the two horses approached and as she did so she once again transformed back into her human form. The two horses also did the same. Their form fading in front of their eyes and then emerging as two beautiful people, radiant and pure, smiles beaming from their faces.

"Rose, we have missed you so much" said Alva as she ran the last few steps and grasped her daughter into a big hug, followed very quickly by Abner who wrapped his arms around them both.

"I've been hoping for this moment for so long" said Rose tears welling up in her eyes.

"Oh Rose, we love you so much" said Abner before turning to Alex. "Alex you have been so brave. We cannot thank you enough. We always knew you could do it and now you've demonstrated that you can turn back from fear to love, there is real hope for everyone in Velaro Fore. We must all return there at once. There is no time to lose and no time to explain. We will first go to the others who are waiting patiently at the house and then we must return to Velaro Fore. There is not much time left."

Gradually they all changed back into their true form as majestic alicorns and Alex jumped again onto Rose's back as they sped through the forest and back into the garden at the house.

Alice was the first to spot them and she almost dropped her coffee in shock as she saw three pink horses with wings and horns in the back garden with Alex riding on one of them. She called all of the adults over and as they came closer to the house they watched them transform back into people right before their eyes.

As they walked through the back door and beckoned them to sit, all of the adults were completely speechless, including Mrs Johnson who just stood there open mouthed. Rose was the first to speak.

"I found them. I found my Mum and Dad. It's them, the King and Queen of Velaro Fore. Alex came to me, when I thought he would be the last person to come back from the crystal kingdom."

"Rose so much has happened, I'm struggling to take it all in" said Alice as she looked round at the others. "Abner, Alva it is so good to meet you but I'm so worried about all of the children and what is going to happen next. Please can you bring them back here."

"Unfortunately that is not something that we are able to do right now, nor can we guarantee that we will be able to" began Abner. "The only thing that we can do is return to Velaro Fore at once and hope that Rose is ready to help us to set them free. This is not something that she can do alone. She needs all of us to come, including all of you."

"You mean we need to come with you to Val...Velire..." asked Alice looking even more shocked.

"Velaro Fore," Abner corrected her.

"All of us?" asked Anthony, clearly uncomfortable with the idea.

"Yes" continued Abner. "If we are going to overcome Nerrez and Maura we are going to need all of the help we can get and Rose will need your support. I'm afraid there is no time to lose. You must come with us and you must come right away. We have one last portal crystal with us. The combination of this and the Rainbow Tiara will take us all to Velaro Fore immediately and you will all become your equivalent magical animal. Together we can prove ourselves too strong for our enemies. Are you ready to come with us and fight for our freedom? For your children?"

"Well when you put it like that" said Anthony looking around at the others, "there is only one answer. We will all do anything for our children. So come on let's go!"

Abner nodded and placed the final portal crystal on the ground and it started to glow. The crystals in Rose's tiara started to glow and a great beam of light shot up into the air and one by one they all began to change into animals and floated instantly, heading back into the crystal kingdom.

Chapter 21 - United Again

Sunny and Eden were in the middle of the counsel chamber with all of the other animals when they heard a rumbling in the distance followed by a bright beam of light that shot straight through the roof of the chamber. Everyone froze, fearing the worst when they quickly realised that they had nothing to fear at all.

In front of them was quite honestly the greatest sight they could have wished for. Their rightful King and Queen had returned. They were right there before their very eyes, radiant and regal and they had brought with them Rose, Alex and some new visitors.

"Your majesties" said Sunny, bowing before them. "We have all prayed for this day and for your safe return. This truly is the greatest moment that we could have wished for. I never doubted that you would come back. Not for one second and now here you are."

"Oh your majesties it is so amazing to see you" called out Eden. "So much has been happening but we felt your presence stronger and stronger in this last day. We're so proud of Rose and Alex and the other children for being brave and strong enough to allow you to come this far. Who else is this with you?"

"This is Alice and Anthony, Rose's adoptive parents who as you can see are now horses. Also, Kel and Christophe are Callum, Violet, Ruby and Alex's parents. Kel has become a lion and Christophe an eagle too just like Violet. Lucy is Issy's Mum and she has become a deer too and Mrs Johnson is a very important lady who has been helping us ever since we left Velaro Fore and she has also become a deer" said Abner pointing them out one by one.

"Nerrez and Maura will know straight away that we have arrived" added Alva looking at Abner as if to remind him of the pressing nature of things.

"Alva is right" said Abner. "Everyone please listen to me very carefully. There are many things that we both want to say to you but right now there is no time. We will just have to limit all we have to say to a massive thank you for everything you've all done and how you have stood firm while waiting for us to return. We have one more battle ahead of us. One which we cannot lose. We will leave immediately and we will no doubt meet Nerrez head on the battlefield. There won't be much time and we will be outnumbered severely. Nevertheless we have Rose with us and she will provide us with the key to victory. We have waited all of this time for her to be ready for the task ahead. When the time comes, we know she will not let us down." Abner looked at Rose and everyone was staring at her. She was quite sure that she didn't know what to do but had a growing confidence that when the time was right something would happen and she would receive some guidance somehow. She nodded at Abner, her father and he turned back to the crowd.

"Our loyal friends, tonight we will face our greatest enemy of all. Our Fears. We will stare it right in the face in the form of Nerrez, Maura and all of their hordes. Remember, they all once loved us and we once loved them. Let us have the strength to rid our land of this darkness. Together we stand, together we shall prevail. Let us go, we have no time to waste!"

"Everyone, let's go!" shouted Sunny.

"We all stand together" shouted Eden and they all turned and poured out of the counsel building and off into the night, towards the dark palace to face Nerrez once again.

Nerrez of course had been waiting. He hadn't expected them to return so fast but he had known that something was happening ever since Alex had slipped out through the portal crystal earlier that evening. He had felt the portal activate and knew that it was Abner and Alva's doing. As soon as he felt it he went into Maura's chambers and told her that they were to prepare the army once more and that they were to bring the prisoners with them onto the battlefield.

They had been lying in wait for them now for several hours. He was determined to make swift work of this. There were so many of them that he knew that when those pathetic loyalists saw them they would start shaking with fear and the victory would be his. It was just a question of taking care of Abner, Alva, Rose, Sunny and Eden once and for all. Even if they didn't turn he would take them captive and they would have to live out their days serving him. Either that or he would banish them again to another dimension, this time to one not so pleasant. Whatever happened he was ready.

Any moment now they would come into sight at the top of the mountain. They would see him down below with all of his power and all of his army and they would tremble, he just knew it. Yes, there they were. He could see them now coming into view. There were even less than he thought and he just laughed again to himself.

"This is going to be too easy" he muttered as he looked across at Maura. She looked like she was still not speaking to him but he couldn't have cared less. She'd come around soon enough once they'd taken over every last one of them. Once he had rid them all from this place she would have no choice but to worship him, just as everyone else did and she knew it.

Nerrez watched them coming down the mountain, gradually getting closer. They didn't seem to be slowing down in any way. Surely they weren't going to just keep on going. They didn't stand a chance. But that is exactly what they did and eventually they marched right up to Nerrez and faced him head on.

It was Nerrez who made the first move sending in his first wave of attack. There must have been ten thousand troops who immediately sped forwards from his army towards them.

Abner and Alva stepped forward along with Rose, followed by Alice, Anthony, Sunny, Eden, Morgan and the other remaining horses, all of whom were now unicorns. As Nerrez's troops came closer Abner started chanting and they all drummed their hooves into the ground.

"You are the masters of your fate. Change is within you." Abner chanted over and over again as they drew closer and closer before suddenly stopping right in front of them.

Rose looked around amazed and suddenly she knew what to do. A strong glow came from Rose and all of the other horses, their enormous graceful wings stretching out on either side of them. Rose was the first to step forward and as she stretched out her wings and wrapped them around one of Nerrez's troops. The effect was instantaneous on all of them. They all changed right before their eyes. No longer were they dark, grey, dangerous and gripped with fear. They had turned back into their true nature and true form and were bathed in love and grace. It was though they had woken up from a deep sleep but in just a few seconds they realised where they were and that they were being led by their true king and queen.

Nerrez was enraged and immediately called upon another wave of attack this time with a much larger group, close to one hundred thousand. Again they ran at full speed with their heads down snarling, looking dark and scary. Once again Abner began the chanting and started to drum his hooves on the ground and this time all of the loyal ones joined in and the noise was terrific.

"You are the masters of your own fate. Change is within you" he chanted and the others all joined in. They chanted over and over again and once again the same thing happened, as the troops drew closer they stopped right in front of them.

Her confidence rising Rose stepped forward along with all of the others and they each spread their wings around one of the dark troops. Instantly they changed back into their true form and again now fell into alignment with Abner and Alva's troops.

With almost half of his army out of action within the first couple of minutes of the battle, Nerrez suddenly became desperate. Those remaining of the dark troops remained glued to his every word and awaited their orders to attack but Nerrez had other ideas.

"Bring me the prisoners one by one" he screamed at Maura who had been standing with them. "Maura, bring the dragon first. We'll make an example out of him." Maura was in a state of shock but managed to order her guards that surrounded the cage that the children were inside to open it and pull George out. He stood there looking at Maura wondering exactly what was going to happen next as she reached down to him. That was when he noticed the hesitation in her eyes and he took his chance.

"You are the master of your own fate. Change is within you" he whispered. Maura looked at him stunned.

"Have you lost your mind" she spat back at him. "He will kill us both."

"You are the master of your own fate. Change is within you" he repeated. "I'm not scared of him. You needn't be either. It's ok."

"Maura, bring him to me now" screamed Nerrez. "RIGHT NOW!!"

"I am the master of my own fate" whispered Maura.

"Look!" said Rose to Abner and Alva.

"Something is happening."

What happened next really became a bit of a blur as it happened so fast but George lurched forward to Maura and wrapped his wings around her as Nerrez struck out using his crystals. A dark beam shot out with George taking the full impact and falling to the ground. Everyone held their breath as George remained motionless on the floor with Maura inside his wings. A few seconds passed which seemed like an eternity and then gradually Maura began to emerge. She was no longer twisted and grey and hideous though. She was beautiful, graceful and radiant with love. She leant down and put her hand out to George's heart, a soft light enveloped him completely and then quickly faded. George opened his eyes and stood up.

"You saved me" said George looking at Maura and seeing how she had transformed before his eyes. Maura turned and walked towards Nerrez who had fallen completely still.

"You are the master of your fate. Change is

within you" she called out to him as he stood rooted to the spot. Everyone started chanting the same words and stamping their hooves into the ground as Maura walked closer and closer. One by one all of the dark army were changing back into their true form until Nerrez was the only one left. He looked at Maura and at all of the troops surrounding him and shook his head throwing the portal crystal to the ground.

"Never!" he cried at the top of his voice as a portal opened up in front of him and he jumped straight into it, taking the portal crystal with him. He was gone.

Maura looked around in shock and started to cry. Abner and Alva ran to her to offer some comfort. Rose ran straight over to George and the other children who all just stood together in a massive group hug and before long they were all laughing tears of joy. They had done it, they had won. The crystal kingdom had been saved.

Chapter 22 - Love or Fear

Rose sat staring out of the window back in her pink bedroom. Three weeks had passed since she had left the Crystal Kingdom behind. She had had to make a very difficult choice shortly after the final battle. Stay in Velaro Fore with her true parents Abner and Alva or return to live with Alice, Anthony and George. She really didn't feel capable of making the decision and the longer she had thought about it the harder it had become.

There had been lots of tears and hugs and long conversations and walks but in the end matters were taken out of her hands. That final night back in Velaro Fore they had all gathered together for a feast and a celebration at the return of the King and Queen and the return of true peace to Velaro Fore. It had been wonderful right until the point when her Dad had told her that she needed to make a decision about her future.

"Don't worry Rose, my beautiful princess" he had

said as he looked down at her smiling. "Tonight we will all sleep and when you wake you will know what to do."

And so she had slept and she had dreamed all about her time growing up as a little girl in the village and how happy she had been. All the while with a sense of yearning inside of her to know where she truly belonged. That yearning had now passed. She knew who she truly was and the power that had lain within her for so long. She knew what she was capable of now and when she opened her eyes she was back in the garden and so was everyone else that had gone into the crystal kingdom with her.

It was hard to take at first and hard to adjust. Every night when she fell asleep she had expected to go back into the Crystal Kingdom, but it hadn't happened. She had gone into the woods again with the children to the cave but there was nothing to be found. Even her beloved tiara had gone missing and she just assumed that it had stayed behind in the crystal kingdom. As the days and weeks of their holiday had come to an end, Rose finally had to accept that it was all over. All that she had left were her memories.

It was a calm and beautiful night with a full moon reflecting across the garden and out into the fields. After the long journey back she had expected to have slept all night without waking up but for some reason she just couldn't sleep. So now she was just sitting there staring out and dreaming once again.

She got off the windowsill and walked over to her desk where she had left all of her books that she had read so many times. The cover of one of them caught her eye. It was called 'The Lost Animal Kingdom' and was one of her favourites. Inside the back cover was a long list of other books by the same author.

'Return to the Animal Kingdom. The Talking Lion. The Rainbow Children' were just some of the titles and then there was one more that she had always wanted to read but had never been able to get hold of 'The Land of Love or Fear.' She looked at the title again and it seemed to just jump out at her. Love or Fear. She grabbed a pen and paper and wrote the letters out in capitals.

LOVE OR FEAR

Then she started to rearrange them one by one until they spelled something else.

VELARO FORE.

"Love or Fear. Velaro Fore" she whispered. "I choose Love!" she said a little louder. She looked around her room and knew straight away that it wasn't her imagination, suddenly everything was glowing!

She ran straight downstairs and out through the back door and into the garden, gradually picking up speed. As she came to the tall garden fence she sped up even faster and took a great big jump closing her eyes and as she did so she felt herself lift up into the air upon her majestic wings. She was an alicorn again and was flying across the fields. She circled around and flew back towards the house up to George's bedroom window which was wide open and hovered outside her wings gently flapping.

"George" she called out. "George wake up."

George opened his eyes and looked out of the window with a mixed look of confusion and wonder on his face.

"Rose, how did you do that?" asked George jumping up and running to the window.

"I chose it George. I chose love. It is the secret of the crystal kingdom. We can choose it anytime. I finally understand" said Rose excitedly. "Come out into the garden with me, quickly."

George ran downstairs and into the garden.

"Now just run George and close your eyes and think of love" shouted Rose as she landed down next to him. George started to run across the garden and as he got close to the fence he closed his eyes and jumped. As quick as a flash he had been transformed back into a dragon and was flying up next to Rose. They flew next to each other for a few minutes and then landed on top of a large hill not far from the house.

"We have to tell the others George. We can go back into the crystal kingdom. We can go back and see them all. They are all going to be so excited."

"But how do we get back Rose" asked George suddenly. "We may have transformed but we're still here."

Rose closed her eyes and within seconds a large portal opened up in front of them.

"That's how!" said Rose smiling. "Come on George, what are we waiting for. Let's get the others and go back into the Crystal Kingdom. We must tell them what we've discovered."

"You're right Rose. Let's go!" shouted George and they both jumped into the portal and disappeared in a flash!

Printed in Great Britain
by Amazon